AUDREY'S RISING
A SERIES OF ANGELS SPIN OFF

JOEL CROFOOT

CHAPTER 1

Butator closed the door to his office with a sigh of relief.

Blessed silence at last!

Everyone in Gabriel's estate was nice enough to live with, but their constant yammering and nonsensical musing got old pretty quickly. Disturbingly, no one else seemed to mind it, just him.

In fact, he would go as far as to say they all seemed to enjoy it. All day long they uttered their illogical reflections aloud, and yammered back and forth to each other like they understood the noise; it was as if it was some secret language he wasn't privy to.

Another code he had yet to crack.

Fortunately, Gabriel had allowed him to soundproof this place, although the request had been received as odd. He could tell, because Gabriel's eyebrows had furrowed like they did when he was asking questions.

Thank God, I cracked the code of Gabriel's human-like facial expressions. Furrowed eyebrows equaled confusion, and confusion was synonymous with 'out of the ordinary.'

Which apparently meant the others *enjoyed* the constant sounds of television, radio, or the like.

How weird, he thought. *But since I am the only one who doesn't like these things, I guess that makes me the weird one?* He felt like he was standing outside in the cold watching a happy family through a window that would never open. He sighed, deciding to abandon that depressing train of thought.

He swiveled in his high back chair, as he regarded the three monitors on his desk. He looked at each one in turn, just to ensure all was well. One had surveillance videos that displayed Gabriel's estate, and the Tuscany house, one had his email account, and the last monitor held the current algorithm he'd made that he was testing.

Numbers had always come easily to him, much more easily than people. Numbers were reliable, they made sense. They never lied, they never had double meanings, and they were simple.

People were the exact opposite. Even with good intentions they spoke falsely quite frequently, and worse he was expected to understand when they were doing so. Like the time when Jahi said she was fine, and he took it at face value, only to get punched in the arm by one of his brothers. *How was I supposed to know she wasn't fine, if she said she was?*

Hamal had tried to explain the tone, body posture, and facial expression combination, but that failed to account for too many variables to him, as though everyone was playing a game, and making up new rules as they went.

Despite being alone in the room, he grimaced at the memory. *Anyway, back to work.*

He clicked on one of the emails from yesterday that Gabriel had sent with the comment, "Can you look into this for me?"

It was from a local lesser angel, a male that he recognized as the one who was undercover as a human in the Los Angeles Police Department. Butator opened the attachments. They appeared to be screen shots of a bank account, going back three years. Listed in green were cash deposits coming in, and in red were large amounts being transferred to another bank. He shifted to another computer beside him and typed in the receiving bank's information, revealing a bank in southern Mexico.

He glanced back at the original email from the LAPD officer, and finally read the message.

Hi Gabriel,

We did a wellness check on a 92 year-old man with Alzheimer's yesterday, he was fine, but while we were there, I was able to flash around the house undetected by my human partner. I found these bank statements, but according to the human rules I wasn't supposed to go snooping around the house without probable cause, so I can't report them to our police department.

How is a 92 year-old man depositing so much money every day from different locations in the city? He can barely even walk, let alone drive. I don't think he has any family other than the live-in care-taker.

Yes, that is suspicious. He was alone in the room, but Butator nodded his head anyway, in his attempts to practice human mannerisms.

He re-opened the attachments, this time noting the locations of the deposits, and began marking them on a map, just like Jahi had taught him to do when he'd first arrived on earth and they were looking for Agares.

Hours later, his phone vibrated, signaling to him that it was time for dinner.

* * *

Audrey sat down at the dinner table, surrounded by some of the most powerful angels in the heavenly host, and a few adopted demons like her. Across from her sat her grandfather Barakel, Angel of Lightning, whom she'd only met last year despite her four hundred years of demon-hood. Next to him sat his partner, one of her former demonic acquaintances Philotanus, Demon of Sodomy. It was in an effort to get to know her grandfather and for him to acknowledge that she was still here, living with angels.

She looked around to confirm, as she did every night, that she was not in some weird dream. But then Asael joined them at the table with his wife, the healer - Isda, little miss fucking perfect herself. As usual, he avoided all eye contact with Audrey as he sat down, and her mood soured.

She was surrounded by plentiful steaming food, a loving family, and living in Beverly Hills, but she couldn't outrun her past. Asael would always steer clear of her when possible, but she understood. He was ashamed of his past and how they'd met in a BDSM sex club, with her as the submissive.

Because I'm the kind of person people are ashamed to know.

Did Isda even know that was how they'd met? Did Isda know how much Audrey hated her?

Asael was well aware.

Hell, she'd practically thrown herself at him, only to be turned down cold for this perfect little American Girl doll, who probably thought the world ran on rainbows and puppies.

Ugh.

Audrey picked up her fork, ready to eat and run back to her room as usual, and dived into the pasta in front of her, barely listening to the conversation.

In some ways, she was grateful to be here. The security was wonderful and she had family here, it's just that she knew this was all a farce and she couldn't let herself get attached. She was the least rehabilitated of the demons. Everyone else clung to this hope that she would rise to ranks of angel someday, like Michael's wife, Jahi, was doing.

Audrey knew better though. She wasn't rising, now or ever. She would never be good enough. Hell, she wasn't even sure she wanted to be. She sure as hell didn't want to start acting like Miss Priss at the other end of the table.

"What do you think of this Audrey?" she heard Gabriel ask, pulling her out of her thoughts.

She tried to replay the conversation mentally in her head to catch up. "I'm sorry, I wasn't paying attention. What do I think of what?"

She watched as every head turned to Butator, who sat stoically looking at the table in front of him. He was strange, even for an angel with his dorky, Asperger-like characteristics. Like all the angels he was muscular from fighting practice, exercise, and she supposed God's grace, but his bright red hair did nothing to detract from his nerdiness.

His face didn't move, save for his mouth, as he spoke. "I looked at a bank account that an angel in LAPD found, under the name of an elderly man with dementia. Every day there are small amounts of cash deposited from different locations around the American Southwest, and then approximately once a week there is a large transfer to an account in southern Mexico."

She shrugged. "It's probably standard money laundering. That's basically how we used to do it," she noted, referring to her life in street gangs.

"What if it's just a family helping loved ones back in southern Mexico?" Isda asked, and Audrey closed her eyes to stop herself eye rolling at Isda's naiveté.

She would think that. She probably fucking believes in Santa Claus too.

"It could be," Gabriel acquiesced, but gave Audrey a look suggesting he had his doubts. "Audrey, would you be willing to work with Butator on this one? I know that gangs were one of your areas of expertise."

Why do I have to get stuck with the fucking weirdo?

She didn't say that though, she just nodded. She knew why she got stuck with the weirdo; it was because she was expendable. They probably didn't think this task was important because if it was, they would have given it to one of the elder angels, not an angeling and a demon at that. They expected her to fail, or at least they didn't care if she did.

At first she was angry at the thought, but in an instant her mind ran through a catalog of stored images: the image of her brother's body being tossed overboard on the slave ship that had brought her the islands - to the broken promise, albeit unspoken, to her parents to watch out for him, - to the baby she'd lost with Zepar, - to the boy in the crack house she'd been too late in finding.

Hell, she expected herself to fail too.

Besides, what good was it to succeed? Was taking out one demon really worth the effort? Another one would take its place, why even try?

Maybe the angels just wanted her to answer more questions. Fine, whatever. It was something to do at least. She nodded her head. "When?"

"Tomorrow, let's start at eight o'clock," Butator added, glancing nervously at her and then back at the table.

"In the morning?" she asked incredulously.

He gave her a baffled look and chuckled like he thought she'd been kidding. Then when he noticed that no one else was laughing, he looked away quickly. "Yes."

Oh for fuck's sake... "Fine."

Four hundred years in hell and they want me to babysit their fucking rain man. Well, at least that should be a job I can't fuck up.

CHAPTER 2

"These are the locations of the money drops," Butator informed a yawning Audrey, who gave the map only a cursory glance; much to his dismay. She had her long dark braids pulled back into a ponytail, and had brought a cup of coffee with her.

Perhaps he wasn't emphasizing the importance enough. "It's every few days at the ones in red and once a week at the ones in green."

"Isn't that festive?" she spoke dryly.

"What is?"

She tilted her head to the paper. "The map."

"The map?" he repeated in genuine confusion. "It's merely a small visual representation of the southwestern United States. How could it indicate festivities?

"The colors, red and green, like Christmas," she said smirking, but he wasn't sure why.

"No, they're to mark the frequency of the money deposits," he told her again.

She snorted. "I got it, I was making a joke."

He considered the colors, but couldn't find anything

funny about it. Blue was a Christmas color too. Maybe he should have used different colors but there were only so many highlighters.

"Forget it," she added, taking a seat.

Butator decided to take her advice and move on from this puzzling detour about colors. "This is the bank where the money is being deposited." *Did the color yellow have any significance?*

She leaned in to see the map of southern Mexico, scrutinizing the location. "If the money is going to a demon down there, there are quite a few in the area. It's basically a hotbed of demonic activity. Who is withdrawing the money?"

"I don't know. I'll try to hack into their surveillance cameras and banking system to find out."

"Do you want me to just go down there and wait to see?"

He pinched his lips together. That was a dumb idea, but Jahi had told him that it was impolite to point it out when he thought so. "I will hack into their cameras and banking system. There is no need to expose yourself."

He turned to the computers and began clicking away to do just that.

It felt strange having someone in his office while he was working. It changed the feel of the room, and the smell. She smelled like vanilla or maybe coconut? It made him think of cookies and smiling. There was more though. She smelled like... healthy young women. The smell made his body tingle in places he found quite distracting.

Get back to work.

While he was working she looked around his office in a silence that lasted about two minutes before she asked, "Why don't you put pictures in here?"

Pulled away from his work, he looked up in surprise. "Pictures of what?"

"Things that make you happy," she shrugged.

"Why?"

"I don't know, sometimes they help you think, or if it's a landscape you can pretend you're somewhere else, or just appreciate the talent of the artist."

What a preposterous idea. "If I wanted to be somewhere else, I would go there. Jahi will teleport me anywhere I want until I can do it myself, she said so."

That particular celestial ability probably wouldn't kick in for another fifty to a hundred years, and Butator had only been on earth a handful so far. "Besides, why would I appreciate the artist while I'm working? Wouldn't it be better if I set aside time to consider that?"

"Hey, it was just an idea."

People are weird, reaffirmed of his belief he went back to work. Another minute or two passed before she inquired about what he was doing. "I'm trying to join the control panel of the CCTV, but I need to run a search for their password."

She nodded, apparently appeased, and then she pulled out her own phone to poke at the screen. They sat in silence together as his program ran its course, and he turned his attention to other tasks he'd been assigned.

"Did you find it?" she asked.

"Yes, and now I'm putting an application on their computers to record all of their transactions."

She looked like he'd just told her that he was moving Earth's moon to Mars. "You can do that?"

"Yes."

Her lips parted and her eyebrows rose. "So you can spy on anyone you want?"

"If they use electronic devices, I can."

Immediately she pocketed her phone.

Butator wasn't sure why she looked so surprised. Most angels could spy on people somehow, like cloaking themselves in invisibility. Some demons could even possess people, so what was so special about hacking some electronic devices? Even talented humans could do that.

He turned back to his work while she got up to look out the open window, and silence fell again for several moments. Voices drifted in from the back yard, where it sounded like Asael and Isda were by the pool. Butator was just glad it wasn't him. He wasn't particularly fond of lounging in the hot sun; he only endured the activity when Jahi insisted he needed to get some fresh air.

Finally, Audrey broke the silence without turning away from the window when she asked, "Do you ever wish you could just be someone else?"

Pulled from his task again he pondered this question. "No, I just become who I want."

She spun to face him. "You've never been jealous of anyone?"

It was a broad question and he told her as much. "Jealous of possessions, abilities, appearances?"

"Just... everything," she answered, looking wistfully out the window again.

"Of course not. That's stupid," he declared, determined that this was in fact the only right answer and proud of himself for figuring out this puzzle.

"Well maybe I'm just stupid then!" she snapped suddenly and headed for the door.

He observed her reaction with the confusion he reserved for almost all human behavior, but quickly disregarded his perplexity and placed her in the category of having bizarre tendencies. Returning his attention to the screen, he calmly replied only to her words.

"No, that's not true at all. Your reasoning powers are higher than average, you're perceptive, you learn quickly and retain what you learn, and usually only have to be taught everything one time. Your memory appears to be fully intact too. I don't know why you would say you're stupid, when your cognitive abilities are above average."

Audrey stopped with her hand on the door knob, and then turned to look him square in the eye, making him uncomfortable. Had he said something wrong, violated another of society's nonsensical rules of etiquette?

She moved her lips as though she were trying to make words without sound, until finally she managed to say, "That's... that's the nicest thing anyone has ever said to me."

Relieved that she found these things pleasant, he answered. "Well, it is all true. If the people you hang out with don't tell you this, then you shouldn't hang out with them anymore."

By the shock on her face, one would think he'd just delivered a blow. Her eyes were even beginning to moisten like he had, and she muttered something about having to leave, and then all but fled the room.

Butator stared after her completely baffled. *I said something wrong again.*

Audrey headed down the stairs and towards the back door. She'd teleport from there to the backhouse just to avoid having to walk past Asael and Isda, but right now she was still thinking about that last comment from Butator, the one about the people she'd been hanging out with. She'd been hanging out with demons in hell, compliments hadn't exactly flown. It was actually usually more of a competition of whose words could cut the deepest, when it was only words being used, that was.

Before then she'd spent much of her time as a plantation slave, enduring the master's attention, until she killed him with a piece of the chain he'd once used to secure his slaves. She really couldn't remember the last time someone had referred to her as intelligent, and certainly not so earnestly as this angel just had.

She wasn't sure what to do with this new piece of information.

It didn't fit with what she knew about herself. If it had come from anyone else she would have discounted it as false or intended to manipulate, but this angel was likely the only person on earth who wouldn't (perhaps couldn't) lie.

When she was with the demon horde she would have squirrelled this piece of perception away to use to her advantage somehow, but right now pondering ways to weaponize his fondness for her own advantage made her feel dirty.

She finally gave up trying to make sense of it and pushed the whole thing from her mind, only then realizing she'd walked right past Asael and Isda, without even noticing.

That night, Butator went down for dinner at six p.m. sharp, joining those who showed up early. He was trying to work out what would make someone arrive early for dinner when it didn't change the time the food was served.

When they'd sat down and the first few bites were taken, Gabriel began his typical conversation, asking everyone about their day. Ramatel had killed a demon last night, Barakel and Philotanus were hunting out some horde in San Diego that they thought had ties to the Los Angeles horde.

"And you guys, Audrey and Butator," Gabriel brought the subject around. "How did it go today?"

"Good," she answered.

"And what were you doing?" Gabriel prodded. Audrey looked at Butator, as if willing him to field this question.

"I hacked into the bank while Audrey taught me a game," Butator replied.

She looked confused. "I did?" she asked.

He glanced up but she was staring at him and he looked away again quickly, disturbed by the inspection. Why was she looking at him like that? Was she still mad that he'd told her to stop seeing her friends?

"What was the game?" Gabriel asked.

"Audrey asks a question about a random topic, unrelated to any subject we've discussed before and I have only two or three tries to guess the answer before she tells me and picks a new one."

A momentary silence fell over the table before Audrey burst out in a fit of laughter, so hard she had to hold her stomach. Everyone quickly joined in, and though Butator wasn't sure what they were laughing at, he smiled too, just pleased that everyone was enjoying themself.

Are they laughing at me? Just play along and they'll think you made up a joke on purpose.

At the other end of the table, Audrey was still chuckling moments later and now wiping tears from her eyes, but in that moment, it occurred to him that he'd never heard her laugh until this moment.

Her laugh was delightful, full, loud, and contagious. Her face was flushed and her eyes shone. She looked good laughing and he wanted to see her do it more often.

CHAPTER 3

The next day Audrey rejoined Butator in the office, still sipping coffee but looking slightly more alert than yesterday.

"Good morning," she greeted him.

"Good morning," he answered, looking up from the computer. He tried to smile at her, because he was genuinely glad she was here, and her presence, despite still making him slightly uneasy, now made him uneasy in a way he hadn't felt with anyone else before. He'd decided yesterday that he liked her being here.

He liked the smell of her, and looking at her, and the way he felt when she looked at him. He jumped at his own train of thought.

"How's it going?" she asked, standing in the center of the room.

"How's what going?" he asked, suddenly nervous as if she'd read his mind.

Momentarily befuddled, she answered with, "The money trail search."

Relieved, Butator clicked open another window and

checked on it. "The money is still in the account. I have an alarm set to alert me if something happens."

"Oh okay, should I leave you to it until then?"

Butator paused at this question. "Do you want to wait somewhere else?"

Her eyebrows rose. "Um, no, no, I just don't want to disturb your work."

"You're not disturbing me," he replied, confident that was a reassuring comment, then went back to his work.

Several more moments passed in silence while he waited for her to start the question game again. Maybe she was thinking of more questions.

"Do you want me to wait here?" she asked.

Is this the beginning of the game? "Yes."

She narrowed her eyes and worded the next question carefully, as though she could taste the sound as it left her lips. "Why?"

Butator stopped typing and chanced a brief second of eye contact. "Gabriel told us to work together and you know the most about demon horde gangs..." He glanced up to see her posture had shifted. Her shoulders were lower than before. *That must have been the wrong answer.* He quickly shifted through other reasons that he'd wanted her here, "...and, because I like you."

"What?" she asked, incredulously.

Perhaps her ears are clogged. He started to repeat the whole thing louder this time but she cut him off.

"What do you mean you like me?"

"Your company is enjoyable," he said, wondering if this was some new game, or a slightly different version of the same one from yesterday.

She only stared at him with wide eyes.

* * *

Audrey had no idea what to say or even where to begin processing a statement so simple, yet so deeply complex for someone like her. She swallowed hard, still staring, part of her waiting for him to start laughing or follow it up with an insult, but even as she waited she was aware of the impossibility of that happening.

This angel was different to the other angels, and even from most demons and people that she'd ever met. His genius was undisputed and matched only in quantity by profound... weirdness.

After only four years on earth, he was a fully grown adult male with red hair and a muscular body, and in the two years she had known him, he'd barely uttered more than a dozen words to her. Any conversation she had witnessed between him and others was either work related or riddled with so much technological jargon she couldn't keep up.

Now the weird nerd had just stated that he found her company enjoyable.

Her, the *demon* who lived in the back house! The *demon* who'd trailed Asael here on some school girl crush, the *demon* who'd tried to entice the local horde leader as her lover and failed at that too, the *demon* who was only here because she was Barakel's granddaughter, and he was surely bound by guilt alone.

Her.

But he had to have meant it, so she did the only thing she could think of as an appropriate response to the statement. She smiled, and sat down.

* * *

Hours later, the speakers of the computer chirped and

Audrey saw Butator clicking fervently. "Someone is accessing the account!"

She moved to stand behind him, peering at the camera images, while he pointed to another screen that contained the account activity, and then he sniffed the air in her direction, before he turned back to the screen. "They're making a withdrawal."

He is so weird.

The screen displayed five bank tellers, each with their own customers, and one line of waiting people behind a velvet rope.

"Do you know which one it is?" Audrey asked.

He shook his head. "No, we will have to see who leaves with money."

Soon, a man in a gray business suit who'd been at the middle teller station walked away with an envelope. He was followed immediately by another customer dressed in jeans, a t-shirt, and sneakers who'd been with the next teller.

"Fuck!" Audrey cursed. "Can you follow either of them with cameras?"

Butator began rapidly clicking, and then typing, switching back and forth until a new screen popped up displaying the front of the bank. She could see now that the bank was like its own little compound, the parking lot and building enclosed within a wall, broken only by a gate that led to the street. The suited man exited the gate and turned right, while the t-shirt gentleman turned left. This was going to take in-person-dirty-work.

"I'll go down there. Can you find me a place to land?"

Again his fingers went flying across the keyboard. "Here," he pointed to some decorative shrubs under a flagpole, "but we'll have to be careful when we land and make sure we are lying down."

"We?" she asked.

"You and I," he clarified in all seriousness as he stood up and stepped toward her. "It's my case too."

She didn't have time to argue so she sighed. "Okay, ready?"

"I am ready," he answered robotically, and she put her hands out to grip his biceps, which were quite surprisingly harder and bigger than they should be on a computer geek. Closing her eyes, she teleported them there, concentrating on their positioning to put them in the right place.

As soon as she reformed, she fell on his chest, unaccustomed to transitioning from standing to lying down. They were on green grass, under some bushes, and damn if she didn't notice that his chest muscles were rock hard too.

Holy shit, Audrey, you need to get laid if you're checking out the resident nerd. She pushed that observation aside as she rolled off him.

Just as she was sitting up he caught her wrist. "Wait, go Hispanic."

She nodded her agreement and instantly changed human forms as he did too. His hair and skin darkened as his cheekbones rose slightly and his freckles disappeared.

She wasn't sure she liked this look on him. His dork-factor seemed to fall a little and she pinched her lips in disapproval.

He didn't quite look like him.

As she considered this, he stood and held a hand out to help her up. "Let's go."

CHAPTER 4

"We should split up and each follow one of the men," Butator pointed out.

"No," Audrey answered. "I'm not leaving you alone down here."

What does she mean by that? Does she not trust me or the location? "It makes more sense," he countered, as they jogged toward the sidewalk from inside the bank compound.

"Gabriel will kill me if anything happens to you. We'll follow the suit, and if we're wrong we'll do this again next week."

Butator wanted to protest but she grabbed his wrist and started pulling him down the sidewalk. "C'mon!"

He knew how the others felt about him, always putting him behind them in a fight, always trying to find excuses to leave him at home. Gabriel tried to tell him that they were protecting him because they needed his skills, but there was more to it than that. Jahi used more pet names for him, like 'honey' and 'dear.' They talked to him like he was apt to shatter.

Did Audrey think of him that way too? He hoped not.

He'd meant what he said about liking Audrey, but there was more to it. He'd been giving it a healthy dose of consideration all morning and he decided that he wanted to know what it was like to kiss her. He'd seen kissing on television and read about it. Up until the last couple days he'd always found the behavior strange and unsanitary, but now, imagining the proximity, being so close, touching her, feeling her soft skin…

Now isn't the time to think about that!

The suit was two blocks away already and they walked as briskly as possible without actually running to catch up. The man in question held a determined pace, weaving through the side streets, occasionally stopping to wipe sweat off his brow with a handkerchief. The crowded streets were filled with pedestrians shopping and the locals selling fruits and vegetables in wheelbarrows and carts that created obstacles on the sidewalk, but when Butator tried to walk in the road, Audrey tugged him back, just as a cement truck hurtled by. The noise of it all was overwhelming.

Finally, the man turned into a steep, gravel lined, winding, driveway. There was a fairly steep incline, and at the top sat a mansion, sitting behind a metal gate connected to a twelve foot cement wall. The grounds backed up to the jungle and trees lined the property, obscuring some of the view from the street.

They'd come close to the entrance of the drive, keeping in the shadow of the street trees. Audrey was a couple of paces in front of him. She tugged his arm, drawing his attention. He glanced up at her, long enough to follow her gaze to a camera covering the street.

Perfect! I hope that is easily hackable. Wondering if he could find more he started up the driveway, and was halted about a foot and a half upward. A glance down at the gravel revealed an angel ward barring his path. He pretended to cough heartily, bending over so as to notify Audrey of it, then as if in silent agreement, they both began to back track.

When they'd gone another block in silence he turned down an alley beside a row of buildings that would block the view of the cameras on the mansion's property, if they even went this far.

"What are you doing?" Audrey asked, following him.

"I want to get another look," he answered, breaking into a trot and pointing to the trees on the hill above the end of the alley. When he reached the dead end, he leapt onto the cement wall that held back the jungle from the city. She joined him momentarily and soon they were hiking their way through the jungle towards the mansion.

They didn't have far to go before they spotted the stockade surrounding the estate and slowed, looking in each direction to assess their surroundings.

"Let's climb a tree," she suggested.

He nodded his agreement and began searching for one that would have the right vantage point. The first one he found had several lines of ants already laying claim to it, and he didn't relish the idea of fighting them for it despite the fact that it offered the best view.

"Watch for cameras!" he called to Audrey who'd grown demonic claws and was scaling a tree like a raccoon.

When he'd monkeyed his own way up, he clung to the trunk of a picky tree, which dangled its branches over the fence. The backyard held a swimming pool and palm trees with sacks hanging from them. He scanned for cameras but the ones he saw weren't aimed at them.

Finding nothing unusual outdoors he squinted into the windows, seeing very little until movement behind the far right window drew his attention. It looked like a closet mirror reflecting the image of a young man sitting on the floor with his arm raised over his head. Something was being used to beat his arm and the man yanked it down, only to be bashed in the head with a heavy object. He collapsed onto the floor, mouth and eyes open, looking at the mirror and for a moment it looked like he saw Butator. For a brief moment the world froze as the man's mouth moved once more, as if begging for help, then another blow struck his temple. Butator watched in horror as the life drained out of the man.

Butator released his grip, not caring that he was falling from the tree, and landed on his back.

"Butator!" Audrey called, trying to whisper. "Are you okay?" She reformed beside him on the ground.

"Did you see that?" he asked, standing up.

"Yeah, I saw you fall."

"No, the man getting killed!"

She furrowed her eyebrows. "No? Where did you see that?"

She wouldn't have seen it, he thought. *The mirror's reflection wouldn't have shown it from her vantage point.*

Disappointed, he merely shook his head. "Let's go home." Was it a coincidence that he was in that tree at that time? Did the Father put him there?

"I'm going to try to hack their security system," Butator told Audrey moments later when they were back in his office at Gabriel's estate. He watched her shift from the Hispanic version of herself to her more natural African version.

"Yeah. It looks like we found the right house," she answered, but still looked pensive. "But we should follow the other guy too just in case. There is a lot of demon activity down there. We could have just found one accidentally."

"It is the right one," he spoke solemnly.

"How do you know that?"

He hesitated for a moment to tell her, wondering if she would say he should have done something to stop it. Then argued the point, mentally reminding himself that he couldn't bypass the angel wards.

"Butator?"

"I saw something." He took a deep breath and relayed the story.

"Wow," was her reply, though she wasn't as surprised as he'd been. "Yeah, sounds like the right place."

"It felt like I was put there to see that, like that man was asking me for help," he explained.

She shrugged. "Anything is possible. Seems mean to put you somewhere where you can't help though."

He was already focused on the computers in front of him, trying to get more information about the place and the fate of the man, until he noticed her staring longer than usual.

"What is it?" he asked, hoping he hadn't misread a cue again.

"You just don't look like you," she answered.

He looked down and noticed that his skin held a darker hue than usual and he instantly shifted.

"Better," Audrey told him, and then headed for the door. "Want some coffee?" she called back and he declined.

It wasn't until she was out the door and he replayed his interactions as he tended to do in his search for cues, or as he preferred to think of them, algorithmic anomalies, that he noticed that she'd said 'better,' without him asking what she preferred.

Was that her version of a compliment or just her stating her preference? Why would she even have a preference?

He considered this while his programs were running, comparing her Hispanic version of herself to her as he knew her, and decided that he too preferred her natural version, but then again, he really hated change. He decided to tell her about his preference when she returned, just as she had told him.

* * *

"Find anything?" she asked, when she walked back in ten minutes later.

"No, but I too prefer your natural form to your Hispanic version."

She stared at him, so he felt like he should elaborate. "I like Hispanic people, but I like you the way I met you."

"Okaaaa, thanks."

Did I say something wrong again? No, why would it be alright for her to state her preference and not me?

"How long do you think it will take?" she asked, gesturing to the computer.

"Probably hours, could be days if they have good cyber security."

"OK, I'll check back in later."

When she'd left he returned to work and found that he missed her presence, even though she did take him away from his tasks. It was a strange sensation to get used to someone being there, then to have them suddenly not there.

They'd only been working together for a couple days, but already he missed her when she wasn't there.

***

That night, Audrey lay awake in bed. Sleep was often elusive to her, especially since her brain decided to use this time of day to go through a running list of memories of every time she'd been wronged, embarrassed herself, wished she'd said something, wished she hadn't said anything, and anything else it could produce to ensure that she did not get her beauty rest.

Tonight was different however.

Tonight she was thinking about Butator, and more importantly, the way he made her feel. Something in her gut suggested that if she'd spent her last four hundred years with him, she wouldn't have had that running list of 'should-haves, would-haves, could-haves.' He wasn't the kind of person that put others down, even when they couldn't keep up with his mental figures.

In truth, it was kind of hot.

He was kind of hot, in a totally adorable but secretly lethal kind of way. He stood at least five inches over her, with broad shoulders - that were hard with muscle, she recalled, smiling at the memory of landing on him. His strong jaw and pouty lips contrasted with his pasty white skin and red hair giving him a unique combination between little boy and strong man.

Sure he was weird, but she was starting to appreciate weird. Weird was a cut above the rest apparently.

Her imagination led her to consider what it would be like to date someone like him, to be able to be herself without put downs, without judgement. Could she even dare to dream of such a life?

She shouldn't, she knew better. She didn't deserve it.

An unbidden list of all her errant moments flashed through her mind like a video on repeat. She had existed for four hundred years by being evil. Evil was what she knew and she was good at it. *You want someone dead? I'm your girl. Beaten but alive, just tell me how long to keep them for.*

She'd learned from the best too. She'd survived the seasoning process for slaves in the Caribbean. She'd been well aware of how to break someone's spirit and body before she took up the whip herself in the depths of hell.

So yeah, she knew better then to dream of happily ever after. That was reserved for perfect little angelic prom queens like the one down the hall.

She rolled over, wiping away tears at the disappointing conclusion she'd come to. Her soul would only ever be evil.

CHAPTER 5

Butator let all his programs run, day and night, finding passwords and by-passing security codes. He really did have to hand it to whoever managed the cyber security for the demonic mansion. They knew what they were doing.

Sometimes Audrey came in to check on him. Currently she was reading in the corner and he was glad to have her there, even if she couldn't contribute.

"What are you smiling at over there?" she asked.

He actually hadn't realized that he had been, and he had to consider his work. He'd just found a new encrypted file. Did that make him happy?

No.

What then?

He typed his next few words and hit enter successfully decrypting it and yelled "Yes!" with excitement.

Am I smiling? He touched his cheeks to confirm and found that he was indeed beaming. "I'm in," he explained, and then paused as he considered his next words. He didn't like to leave her question unanswered and he'd been smiling before he knew he had been able to hack into their system, so that was not it.

"I was smiling because it was a good challenge and I think I knew I would win," he explained.

She smiled and walked up behind him. "I doubt there is anything that you can't hack." She put a hand on his shoulder as she peered over him at the screen.

A warm, light hearted feeling swelled in his chest at the honest compliment, and he was keenly aware of her touch. "Thank you." He wanted her to keep her hand there but she removed it.

Together they began scrolling the cameras he'd accessed one by one, noting layouts, counting people, and generally taking stock of the mostly empty rooms in the mansion. A few staff sporadically did some cleaning, but there was no sign of…

Wait!

"Is that a jaguar?" she asked, incredulous.

He expanded the video of a room displaying a large cat lounging in a sunny atrium whose door opened to the jungle that the house backed up to. A massive jade mask hung on the wall behind it and there appeared to be a sort of water canal running through the floor of the room.

The cat lifted its head and looked off screen as if it had been called to attention by something, then it stood. Once up, its body began growing taller, hair receding, arms shortening, until in a moment a man with both African and Hispanic looking features stood on the spot where the cat had been. He had a round head with a wide face and high cheekbones, but somewhat crossed eyes. Then he walked out of view.

"Holy shit!" Audrey exclaimed.

Butator clicked through the cameras quickly, pulling up another from a different angle. The man was now standing in front of a solid metal door, pushing numbers on a keypad, and then he pushed the lever-style handle down and disappeared into a vault.

* * *

That night they all gathered in Gabriel's office for a meeting, rather than the collective dinner meal because some of the angels hadn't yet returned. Now assembled in the study with its leather furniture and rows and rows of books, even a door to a vault where ancient scrolls were kept, they more or less circled Gabriel on sofas and overstuffed chairs.

Audrey sat with Butator, while her grandfather Barakel hovered beside her at the couch, glowering at her new partner. "I can't believe you went down there without telling anyone!" Barakel admonished, mostly to Butator.

"You guys leave all the time without telling anyone," Butator stated flatly.

"It's different for us, honey," Jahi, the risen demoness and wife of Archangel Michael, answered. "We've been around the world, we know how things work."

"You've only been up here a little longer than me this time around and I didn't go alone," Butator answered again. "I'm not a child."

"What if you'd been hurt?" Michael posed.

"Audrey would have transported me back here."

The room went silent and Audrey could tell the real problem had just been exposed. The angels didn't trust her, except for Barakel, who wanted to keep her in a protective bubble. None of them had the balls to say this to her face of course, so they let an uncomfortable silence fill the room instead.

Audrey's mouth also parted slightly as she heard what had just happened. Butator had defended her with complete faith in her abilities, probably more faith than she had herself. Maybe he was too young to know better.

"So what did you find?" Gabriel asked.

Butator leaned forward and clicked a few windows and buttons on his laptop. He hit play on the video and the room fell silent as they all stared at the screen. Collective murmurs began when the jaguar started shifting.

"What the…"

"Damn."

"Holy shit!"

When they'd all watched the man disappear into the vault Gabriel turned to Butator. "How long did he stay in there?"

"He's still in there."

"So this is the house where the money is heading to?" Michael confirmed. "Are there any other cameras?"

Butator started clicking around, demonstrating their options.

"Can you move the cameras?" Michael asked.

"Not without giving away that I've hacked them."

"Big place," Jahi commented, looking at some kind of side yard or backyard, between the house and the jungle. "What are those?" she asked, pointing to gray blurs of large objects hanging from a line of trees that bordered the property on the edge of the jungle. "Beehives?"

Butator took a picture with some program then set it to calibrating, sharpening, and enlarging the image.

"Piñatas?" Jahi asked.

"They look like bodies," Barakel offered.

The program continued its work, making the definition more sharp, and revealing other gray shapes hanging from trees.

"They are bodies." Gabriel confirmed as he stared at the screen. "Mummified maybe?"

"They definitely aren't normal bodies," Michael noted. "I would say they were old, but the skin isn't black, and look at how skinny they are, all the loose skin. It looks like they've been drained of blood, not here though, there are no puddles underneath."

"So, we have werecats and vampires?" Audrey questioned. "What is this, a paranormal romance novel?"

"It's never that easy," Gabriel noted, then got up and went looking for a book in the library, while everyone else continued studying the screen. He returned in a minute with a large dusty hardback book. "I think I may have dealt with this once. Look." He set the book down on the coffee table and opened it to a specific page with a picture on it. The image held something that at first glance looked like a giant mosquito with a monkey-like body.

"Abúhukú," Barakel read aloud. "Rainforest demons, that cut a hole in the skull before they suck out the contents of the body. Occasionally, they roll the prey in palm leaves to tenderize them first."

"Maybe that explains what this is," Michael tapped the screen over a green oblong mass hanging behind the body.

Barakel continued to read. "They are allied with the race of jaguar demons, intent on decimating the human population."

Gabriel looked up as if he suddenly recalled something, and he looked at Michael. "Didn't we flood them out last time?"

Michael stared at him. "Maybe you did. I've never heard of them before. You were probably with Anachel, not me."

Gabriel nodded, half listening. It was easy to miss details like that after a couple thousand years.

"So what are they doing up here?" Audrey asked.

"Good question," Gabriel replied. "You and Butator

try and find out. We'll set someone else to watching the screens."

* * *

After the meeting Butator went to his office to retrieve the locations of the money drops and Audrey followed him in. "They'll probably make a deposit at one of these banks in Nevada tomorrow. I'll know which one as soon as they make a deposit."

"Alright, I'll tail them as soon as we find out."

He looked at her incredulously. She was willing to do a stake-out that seemed like a lot of work. *Am I just lazy or am I missing something?*

"We could just slip a tracking device onto them, or maybe I could get their name from the account and hack their electronics if they have any under their name."

Her expression changed, maybe a frown, maybe sad? He wasn't sure.

"Is that wrong?" he asked.

She shook her head. "No, it's just obvious that you don't really need me."

He paused and thought about this. It was true, for this he didn't. "Do you want me to need you?"

She sighed. "Yes and no."

"I don't know how to interpret that response," he answered honestly. "Those are conflicting answers."

She chuckled but he didn't know why, then she spoke, "You're wired a little differently aren't you?"

His mind conjured an image of himself made of wires but he couldn't compute that either. Maybe she didn't know what angels were made of. "I don't have wires. Angels are biologically mostly similar to humans, we just work better."

This too made her laugh. "I know, it's a metaphor for the brain connections," she explained. "I think your brain works a little differently than most."

He felt his shoulder sag at this. He'd known he was different, it was hard not to notice all of the things he was excluded from, all the jokes he didn't get, all the conversations he couldn't follow. "You think I'm weird."

"I think that's a compliment," she added. "Normal isn't always best."

He glanced up to her face to see if she was making fun of him, but he couldn't tell. "Do you mean that?" he asked, with suspicion.

She gave an exaggerated head bob. "Oh yes. Normal is bad."

He smiled and feeling reassured he went to sit at the computers, as she turned to walk out the door.

"You can stay," he called, aware that inviting someone into his space was extremely unusual for himself. "I don't need you for the computer stuff, but you're better at the people stuff when I hack into their systems."

She smiled and walked back into the room.

* * *

The next day, Butator fired off a text to his brother, Hamal. "Can I talk to you? I have some questions for you and Ornias."

Hamal was a water angel, in the human form of a black man with short hair. He had come to earth at the same time Butator had, only a few years ago, but he'd managed to find a relationship with a demon, so Butator was hoping he could supply some advice. Jahi, Michael's wife, would have been the obvious choice being a risen demoness herself, but Butator knew that if he asked her she might go all mother-hen on him.

A knock on the door was the response to his text.

"Come in," Butator called. His brother walked in, followed by his mate, Ornias, an incubus demon, now in the process of rising from demonhood.

"Got your text," Hamal said, sitting down on one of the chairs, while his partner sat opposite him. "What's up?"

Butator closed his laptop and wheeled his chair around the desk to join them in a triangle. "I would like to pursue a romantic relationship with Audrey, but I don't know how to start," he confessed.

Ornias chuckled a little, until Hamal shot him a stern look. "Okay…" Hamal began, "have you asked her out?"

"Out?" Butator repeated. "We went to Mexico together."

"No, like a date. Take her to dinner, something that has nothing to do with work. Make it obvious that the reason you are spending time with her is solely because you like her."

"Oh," Butator answered. "I already told her this."

"Telling people is one thing," Hamal started, "but most need to see behavior match words." He shot a sly smile to his lover as he said that, and then looked back at Butator. "Take her to dinner, take her to an expensive restaurant just to show her that you want her to have nice things, maybe somewhere like that new place that just opened on Sunset," he suggested.

"How will she know my intentions are romantic and not just sustenance?"

Ornias smirked. "Oh, she'll know."

Butator gave him a confused look at this lack of

answer. *Maybe he didn't hear the first part of the question.* "*How will she know?*"

Ornias gave him a perplexed expression in response as though Butator had just answered in Chinese, so Hamal fielded this one again. "It's a human tradition to ask someone to an exclusive meal to begin a potential romantic relationship. She is probably already aware of this tradition."

Satisfied, Butator nodded. "Then what?"

"Then at dinner, you two talk and see if sparks fly," Ornias answered.

Butator imagined a dinner interrupted by flying metal shards, red with heat. It seemed more dangerous than romantic. Was this another human tradition? "Why would there be sparks at dinner?"

Hamal turned to Ornias. "He doesn't really do metaphors or colloquialisms yet."

"Yeah, I'm starting to pick up on that," Ornias answered dryly, crossing an ankle over his knee.

Butator sighed with frustration as they talked about him like he wasn't there. "What does it mean that sparks fly?"

"It means that there is interest or attraction."

Butator pictured himself providing a Likert-Scale survey of attraction, with questions such as 'on a scale of one-to-ten how likely are you to pursue intercourse with this person?' but his other attempts to quantify interest for game nights and meals had been met with grumbles and curses from the estate's inhabitants. Maybe there was another way.

"How will I know if there is? Do we just proclaim it at the end of dinner?" he asked.

"I got this one." Ornias declared to Hamal. "It's my specialty." He turned to Butator and said, "When someone is interested romantically they will find excuses to close the physical distance between you, and then begin to make physical contact. At first the contact will seem innocuous, but they are using it to test your interest. If they get closer or touch you, and you are equally interested, then you get closer and touch them with a matching level of intimacy. So if she puts her hand on yours, then a few minutes later you do the same, or touch her arm or something. If she leans an inch or two closer, you do the same."

Butator nodded along as he gathered the information. "OK, for how long?"

"Until she kisses you, then kiss her back."

"I don't know how to kiss," Butator confessed.

"Just do what she does."

Butator considered this mirroring practice for several moments then took the principle and extended it beyond kissing. This might have worked for Hamal and Ornias who were a gay couple, and therefore anatomically the same, but Butator found a major flaw if the theory were applied to a heterosexual couple.

"At some point I have to stop mirroring though, anatomically males and females are different, so I won't be able to just match what she does."

Ornias laughed as though Butator had made a joke, and then added. "Don't worry, by that point either biology will take over, or she will teach you."

Butator clenched his jaw with frustration. Was he going to have to research biology for this?

CHAPTER 6

The next day, Audrey joined him to check up on whether or not he'd been able to track the money droppers.

"Audrey," he spoke as soon as she'd entered. "Will you go out with me, to dinner, tonight, at the new restaurant on Sunset? I have reservations."

Whoa! That was not what she was expecting and she froze for a moment, considering. He was asking her out, like on a date. Did she want to?

Yes.

Is there something wrong with me for wanting that? He was only like 4 years old, but he was also a grown man, or angel rather. Everyone treated him like a child, and in some ways he reminded her of one, but with what she had seen in the last few days, her mind was changing. He wasn't retarded; he didn't have the brain of a child, just the opposite actually.

He was a literal genius.

He lived on a whole different level of reality, but it was a higher plane, not a lower one.

What would the others think if she said yes? *Why am I concerned about that? Fuck them.* She hated that she'd even had that thought.

Did she want to? Yes.

And dammit she would.

"Yes," she answered, decisively, already feeling a tingling in her stomach at the idea of a romantic date. She hadn't been on a real date in over a hundred years, not with anyone she truly cared about anyway.

And Butator had chosen one of the fanciest restaurants in Los Angeles. She imagined herself dressed up in a little black dress, with heels and pearls. Wait, she didn't have any of that.

Crap.

"What time is the reservation for?" she asked.

"Six o'clock."

She smiled; of course he wouldn't deviate from the dinner schedule of the house. "OK, but I'll need some time to get ready."

By five-thirty that night, Audrey was dressed in a backless cocktail dress, black nylons, and two inch stilettos with a red decorative flare that matched her newly polished nails and lips. She left her room and headed for the stairs, feeling like a teenager on her prom night. She mentally warred with herself the whole time, going back and forth between the 'This is stupid, why am I entertaining a school boy crush? What do the others think? What would Zepar think?' and 'Who cares what he thinks, you want to go out with him, have fun. The shrink said you're allowed to be happy.'

Am I though? Being happy felt like a betrayal of all those she'd let down in life.

As she descended the steps she was so deep in thought that she almost didn't notice Butator waiting in a three-piece suit that someone had obviously helped him with. He had a fresh haircut, and was staring up at her like she was the most beautiful woman on earth.

Her cheeks actually heated when she saw the way he was looking at her, and despite her internal bickering, she had to admit he looked good. The black suit contrasted sharply with his red hair, and fit around his muscled body perfectly accentuating his broad shoulders and narrow waist.

He looked like he was about to say something when she reached the bottom, but whispers coming from the game room and dining room drew his attention, then hers. Apparently, most of the house had ensured they conveniently had a viewing place for this moment.

Audrey rolled her eyes. "Ready?" she asked.

"Ready, the car is already here."

They rode in a blacked out rented rideshare from the Beverly Hills estate to West Hollywood.

"You look... very... um good tonight," Butator commented as they rode in the back seat. "I mean, not that you don't usually look good, but um..."

As amusing as it was, she decided to take pity on him and stop there. "Thank you. You look good too."

He looked down as though he just realized that he was wearing clothes. He looked back at her, holding her gaze for a full two seconds, probably a record for him. "Thank you. Hamal and Ornias got it for me."

With that established, they both looked out their respective windows, as the dissent in her head grew louder. *I'm old enough to be his third or fourth great grandparent*, one side of her said. *Age doesn't matter among the celestials,* the other side argued. *This is his first date, ever,* one side argued. *He isn't a kid, he is a genius, remember? He just thinks in different ways, but his judgement is his own.*

Her body tensed as she contended with herself, until he drew her out of her internal altercation with a question. "Have you ever been there before?"

She shook her head. "No, I mostly kept to Central and South LA until now," she answered. *The gang territories.* "Have you?"

"No," he answered. "But I don't think they have sparklers there."

Audrey shook her head at the sudden change of topic. "What? No, I doubt it. Why? Did you want sparklers?"

"No," Butator answered. He looked her in the eye again for the second time that night. "But I want sparks to fly," he said with a grin.

Audrey threw her head back and laughed at the first joke she'd ever heard him tell.

They arrived right on time and were greeted at the door by the hostess who looked Audrey up and down, then took Butator's name and waved them to a seating area to wait for their table. Audrey scanned the white linen tablecloths, the candles, the wall of wine racks, black suits, blonde hair, and noticed that she was the only Black person in the place. There were a few other ethnicities represented she thought, Middle Eastern maybe, Hispanic, but no other Black people.

As they waited, others came in, some with later reservations than theirs, and yet they were seated right away. Audrey checked her watch.

"Do you think they forgot about us?" Butator asked.

"No," she answered dryly. "I think they don't like me here."

The look on his face was sheer terror, and he whispered. "Do you think they know you're a demon?"

She snorted as his naiveté. "No, watch." She began to ever so slightly, lighten her skin and shift her hair, noticeable to him, but not likely to the humans. When she reached the point where she presumed humans would think she was a dark skinned Caucasian person, she coughed loudly staring at the hostess.

The young woman seemed a little confused, then checked her papers, and spoke into a radio. Within a minute she approached them. "Right this way."

Audrey began to slowly return to her natural state as they stood.

* * *

Butator followed behind the hostess as she wound her way through tables, but as he walked he could feel a tension building in his chest. He hoped he wouldn't start rocking when they sat down, although he longed to self-soothe because he didn't want Audrey to know how upset he was. *Why would Hamal tell me to bring Audrey to a racist restaurant? Maybe he didn't know, they are new.*

They sat in the booth, indicated by the hostess and waited for her to leave, but a glance at the other patrons was all it took to start him rocking, though he tried to hide it by picking up a menu.

"What's someone like that doing here?" someone on the other side of the room whispered, but his angelic hearing caught it.

Just focus on the menu, he told himself.

"Are you alright?" Audrey asked.

He stopped rocking immediately. *Damn, she'd noticed.* "I don't like it here now I know they're racist," he admitted.

"Do you want me to take you somewhere that isn't?" she asked, and with relief, he nodded.

Together they left the building and walked down the sidewalk until they found a secluded hiding spot in an alley between a wall and a parked delivery truck to disappear from. When they reappeared, they were standing in a similar location, though the make-up of the street had changed and the scent had shifted from dry smog to smoked meat.

He glanced up at a sign that read 'Satdown Jamaican Grill.' They walked to the front, and she led him into a quaint little restaurant decorated brightly in many colors. Rather than waiting for a table however, Audrey approached the counter and placed an order for several dishes to go.

"Aren't we staying?" Butator asked.

She gave him a sly smile. "Nope, we're going on a picnic."

Twenty minutes later, they were alone on top of a mountain, overlooking Los Angeles. "Here we are," Audrey made a gesture with her hand as though she were displaying something. The least racist place in America!"

CHAPTER 7

They ate in silence at first. Audrey seemed to be appreciating the view of the city, while Butator appreciated the view of Audrey. Her skin was as smooth as an ocean rubbed stone, and her small nose turned slightly up. The little black dress had pulled up when she sat, giving him a look at her long slender legs and he wished she wasn't wearing panty hose. He liked her skin, and he wanted to know what it felt like to rub his fingers up and down her legs.

He was even jealous of the chicken being pulled off her fork into her mouth, and he shifted his seating position trying not to give away the physical signs of his envy. He wished he could start a conversation, but his mind had blanked.

"What do you think of the food?" she asked, saving him from himself.

"I like it. We should ask Maria to make it sometime."

Audrey snorted, which he had come to understand meant 'I disagree.'

"You don't like that idea?" he questioned.

"I don't think she could make authentic Jamaican food," she replied, dipping her fork into the curried chicken.

"Maybe she could learn?"

"Nah, for authentic food, you have to go to the source."

That apparently having been decided, they returned to silence again until Butator's phone chirped, and he shot off a reply message.

"What's up?"

He sighed. "Gabriel wanted to know why my location was on top of a mountain."

"What did you tell him?" she asked.

"I told him it's not racist here."

Audrey chuckled a little, then paused and thought. "Does he always check on you like that?"

Butator looked up like he was scanning through something visible only to him. "No, not usually, but whenever I leave I'm typically with my brothers or Jahi."

"So, it's me he doesn't trust then," she concluded.

Butator felt like he should defend Gabriel. "There are other variables in the equation," he answered. "Like it being my first date. Or maybe there are unknown variables, such as a demon attack on someone at the restaurant I told him we were going to."

She pinched her lips and raised her eyebrows. "I doubt it. He's never trusted me, but I don't blame him."

Butator set his food aside. "How come?"

"I'm a demon."

He rolled his shoulders up and back. "So, Jahi is too and he doesn't mind her."

"Jahi is repentant," she answered.

"You're not?"

Audrey shook her head. "Not really. I had good reasons for most of the things I did."

Butator had never pondered that someone might enjoy evil. "So you like being a demon?"

This time she shrugged. "It's really all I've known of the celestial life."

"Why do you stay with us then?" Butator suddenly had a growing fear in his belly that she might leave.

Her expression shifted as if a cloud of sadness had overtaken her. "I'm not very good at being a demon."

He pondered this for a few seconds. "You wouldn't be able to help with the investigation if you weren't," he answered, but quickly added, "but I hope you don't go back to the demons."

Her face brightened at that. "What would you have me be an angel or a demon?"

He looked at her, baffled by the question. "You," he answered. "I would want you to always be authentically you."

* * *

A better compliment could not have been given to her if someone tried, and Audrey felt her heart melt at his words. Someone liked her for her, not for what she could give them, not for her connections, not for a baby as Zepar had tried to use her for, but just herself.

She put the food down and turned to him, planting a kiss on his utterly surprised face. At first he was as frozen as a statue, but she kept her lips on his, then slightly parted her own. He matched her as she slipped her tongue between his, feeling her heart's pace increase, as she found herself falling for him. His tongue slid along her own, in and out, just as hers was doing, a moan escaped her lips, followed by his.

She pulled back, he following her lead, and she was starting to put the pieces together. "Was that your first kiss?" she whispered.

He looked down as though ashamed. "Yes," he answered, and then added. "I think I like kissing though."

A smile crossed her face, understanding that she was going to have to take the lead. "Just wait until you try sex."

"I would like to try sex," he admitted, "with you."

"Good," she practically purred and went in for another kiss. This time undressing him with her hands, as he put his on her sides to steady her as she worked.

"We have to get naked," she whispered in his ear, once he was topless, and they quickly disrobed.

He was muscular and chiseled, she noticed again, but now with a much clearer image. His pale white skin was unflawed, and she noticed, he was well endowed and already excited. The best part was that despite being up here, alone but exposed should some venturous hiker veer off the path, or helicopter do a fly by, he was unashamed. It was liberating, and she reached a hand to stroke his erection.

At the first touch he shuddered and reached out as if he wanted to pull her in, but then stopped just short of touching her like he was afraid that was wrong.

"It's OK," she whispered, "you can touch me."

He put his arms around her, and she pumped his shaft a couple more times, using his white pre-cum to lubricate what she could. Each pump delivered a new shudder through his body and she decided she'd best stop teasing.

"Lie back," she gently commanded.

* * *

Butator did as he was told, disappointed that she'd stopped stroking with her hand, but optimistically hoping that the next step was even better. He'd read about sex and foreplay, but the literature fell short of the acts so far.

His erection ached with need and her hand had helped relieve it, but still he wanted more.

With wonder, he watched as she straddled him, then adjusted his shaft to her entrance. The moment she began to slowly lower herself, he felt a tidal wave of sensation hit him like his body was on fire but an exquisite fire that he yearned for more of.

More!

She grinned at his reaction, and then sank a little lower on him before pulling herself upward and descending again.

Butator felt himself panting. It was like the world had disappeared, the only thing remaining was the warm friction where their bodies connected. He'd never felt so alive, never wanted anything so much. Without conscious thought he began to move his hips with her motion, reaching to support her by the waist. His pace had quickened and he looked up to her eyes for approval. Her own were shut, her mouth hung partly open, and instinctive guttural noises emerged from her lips. Those sounds gave him the unusual sensation of pride and he increased his tempo until he was breathing heavily. He wanted more!

More!

Something was happening in his body. There was an excitement and tension he couldn't resist, like a runaway freight train.

Atop him, clinging desperately to his shoulders Audrey met his rhythm with her body, while the tone of her panting increased higher and higher, until finally the freight train crashed.

A blast of exquisite euphoria sent his muscles rigid and he heard himself groan.

* * *

Audrey pulled herself free of Butator and rolled to the side where she planted herself in the crook of his arm, her head on his shoulder. She was still reeling from the orgasm she'd just had and if she was being honest that might have been one of her best.

It was strange, she thought, having sex with someone she liked, who in return genuinely liked her. No quickie, just for physical joy, but an actual connection.

And she was in control.

That was legitimately new to her. Sure, she'd had sex with demons before where there was a power differential in her favor, but she'd always known it would eventually come around to having conditions.

This was very different and uncharted water to her. She felt like a virgin, learning, and experimenting.

Beside her, he stirred to wipe sweat off his brow and she rolled to study him, his pale skin was tinged pink now with exertion, his full lips twitched into a smile, and he rolled his head her way. She gave him a smile when he made eye contact which he returned but said nothing.

They lay together in silence for several moments until he sat up, and gestured toward the reds and oranges of the sunset.

"It's beautiful," she commented, sitting up beside him and reaching for her clothes.

Butator nodded. "It is, but not as beautiful as you."

She chuckled, presuming the hormone rush of his first orgasm must be tainting his mood, but then she remembered all the other nice things he'd said to her. "Thank you."

Together they dressed, but lingered on the mountain to watch the sun descend over the Pacific Ocean.

"What are you thinking about?" Audrey asked, wondering if he had questions about what they'd just done.

"How to solve racism," he answered. "But without breaking the rules about direct intervention."

She guffawed. "Oh, is that all?" she said, incredulous at the size of the task.

"Yes."

She turned to look at him, of course he was serious! She was about to point out the overwhelming dimensions of the task, but stopped herself.

If anyone could do it, it was him.

CHAPTER 8

A week later found them back in Gabriel's study, along with all the rest of the inhabitants of the estate, save the help of course. It had been a glorious, honeymoon of a week, but there was still work to be done.

Saharial and Heather stood in the back corner, which was Sahariel's favorite place to lurk in his constant attempt to avoid attention as the Angel of Beauty. Barakel and Philotanus, sat on one of the couches across from Asael and his wife Isda. Michael and Jahi were there of course, Michael standing next to his identical twin brother Gabriel, though their expressions couldn't be more different. Anachel, Gabriel's partner, sat with Liwet, and in a few moments they were joined by Hamal and Ornias who'd teleported to the room they kept at the estate and were walking through the door of the cramped study.

"So what have you found?" Gabriel asked Audrey. She'd been tracking the phones of everyone who made deposits, after Butator taught her how. He'd been busy cyber stalking the other person who'd retrieved money the day they followed the suit, then trying to gain more information about the owner of the estate with the jaguar demon.

Audrey shuffled through a stack of papers where she and Butator recorded the locations and stops of each person. "Well, I think one guy is cheating on his wife, but that's basically it." Butator was still clicking away at the laptop on his thighs and didn't look up when the conversation continued without him.

Gabriel turned to look at Barakel and Philotanus who had been down in Mexico following leads about the owner of the jaguar mansion. "And you."

They both shook their heads" "Nothing, but that's suspicious in itself," Philotanus answered.

"How so?"

"The owner's name is Jorge Martinez and his record is squeaky clean. They have money coming in, but in exchange for what? We didn't find drug plantations, we didn't find slaves, we didn't find arms, what are they selling that is paid for consistently with cash? On the surface this guy looks like he owns a few legal businesses, but nothing in the U.S."

"Could be a prostitution ring," Jahi offered.

Barakel picked up his head from where he'd been looking at the floor in thought. "We also still don't know where they got the bodies, or why."

Gabriel rubbed at his face. "I think the why is safe to say for eating." He gestured to the bodies in the pictures that were now shrunken like they'd been embalmed.

Butator set the laptop aside and picked up the papers Audrey had held and began reading through them. He became so engrossed in what he was looking at that he tuned the others out. Audrey had tracked about ten different people, and up until now they'd been looking for a common meeting of all ten or even in small groups. This was the first time he'd considered them individually. As he scanned them, he coded the locations in numbers, like a computer program looking for themes in transcribed interviews or passages.

At the end he mentally tallied the codes, six came up most frequently. *Which one was six?*

Medical clinics.

"Medical clinics," he blurted out, interrupting the conversation and drawing a lot of stares.

"What about medical clinics?" Gabriel asked.

"They're the most frequently coded theme in the records," Butator answered.

Blank stares were the only response.

What the heck is wrong with these people? He thought to himself and tensed his shoulders with frustration as they scrutinized him. *Hadn't they ever heard of factor analysis?*

Audrey put her hand on his and smiled at him. At once the room stopped moving, or rather he stopped moving and everything looked like it was standing still again. Apparently he'd been rocking back and forth.

"You've found something in the locations?" she asked.

"Yes."

She smiled at him. "Tell me what you found, but talk to me like I'm stupid."

Did she still think she was stupid? He didn't want her to think that, and it wasn't true.

"You're not stupid," he said, giving her hand a reassuring squeeze.

Her smile grew but she answered with, "For now, just pretend that I am."

"OK." Butator talked them through his reasoning.

Audrey understood. "So they all visited medical clinics, and that is the most common place shared among them?"

"Yes."

"How did I miss this?" she asked, reaching for the papers to verify.

"They were all different types of clinics, chiropractors, physical therapists, homeopaths, medical doctors, but the common factor is that they're all medical clinics," he explained.

Gabriel looked up as if in thought, then asked, "So what are they offering or selling at these clinics that gets them money to send to Mexico?"

"And how do we find out?" Anachel added in her soft, steady voice.

Heather, the half human psychologist mated to Sahariel spoke up. "I'm licensed in California; I can apply to this one."

"Heather," Sahariel answered in his mild manner. "I don't think that's safe."

"How about this…" Michael stepped into the circle, decisive as ever and demonstrating his planning skills as the Angel of Warfare. "Barakel and Philotanus, you guys continue to watch the Mexican estate, tomorrow everyone else will break off into pairs, each pair taking one location to recon. Get all the info you can and meet back here in two days. Call if something urgent comes up." Then he looked at Heather, the only human among them. "No offense, but I think Sahariel is right. You don't have any celestial skills or healing abilities…" She crossed her arms and scowled at him, which he must have noticed because he quickly added. "And you're the only trained psychologist in the angel world and we can't afford to let anything happen to you.

This seemed to appease her.

* * *

They all met the next day back in Gabriel's study in the middle of the morning to hear Michael assigning sites to couples for them to scope out. Yawning, and nursing a cup of coffee, Audrey listened for her name, but it never came.

Seriously? What the fuck?

"So, what are we doing?" she asked Michael, narrowing her eyes at him.

He looked at her then Butator. "We need you to watch the movements and cameras. Alert us if you see anything."

Audrey fought the urge to roll her eyes. *Was it that they thought of him as a kid or thought she was incapable?* She wondered. *Maybe a little of both.*

She was about to open her mouth to object but in the back of her mind flashed images of all her failures: dead brother, dead child, not bearing Zepar a child, getting captured by Asael... hell, even becoming a demon in general was a failure wasn't it?

She didn't blame them for not sending her.

"Do you have any cameras or listening devices you want us to try to plant?" Asael asked Butator.

Her red-headed lover nodded and left to retrieve something while Audrey crossed her arms in front of her chest and seethed. The others were pulling out their phones and looking up the addresses.

Butator returned and dropped a few tiny microphones on the coffee table. "Get these inside the offices, and hide them somewhere," he told them. "Before you do though, push this button and wait for the light to come on."

The others approached the table, snatching a listening device and holding them in front of their faces to inspect them.

After everyone left, Audrey trailed Butator back to his office in silence, expecting to sit in front of a screen with headphones on.

"Can you believe that?" he barked when the door shut. He paced the room with his hands clasped to the sides of his head.

Her stomach twisted, in all the time she'd known him, she'd never seen him like this. "Believe what?"

"That you and I aren't going! We're the ones who know this case better than anyone, kids could sit here and listen for clues."

She nodded and hung her head, disappointed that Butator was being punished for her shortcomings. "Butator, I don't think this has anything to do with you."

He quit pacing back and forth. "How come?"

She sighed, sad that she finally had to confess to him the truth about her. "They know I'd fuck it up."

He looked genuinely perplexed. "Like, they think you'd sabotage the plan because you're a demon?"

"No, I'm just... I'm not who you think I am," she whispered, feeling her lip quivering.

"You're not?"

She shook her head. "No. I'm just a failure and they know that. I was captured by my own ineptitude that got my brother killed. I tried to escape that plantation so many times. When I tried to kill the owner I killed his whole family too. I've led countless failed missions in the pit, and the only reason the angels found me is because I failed at staying hidden, I even failed at having a baby, and at..." She stopped short of saying 'seducing Asael.'

Even though she'd cut herself off, it actually felt good to say all of that out loud, like vomiting a poison that had been infecting her for a long time, and like any proper purging, it was scary too. She held her arms wrapped around herself, and her hands shook as though she was cold, but the temperature was fine. She wasn't shaking from a physical cold, but long term deprivation of emotional warmth.

Audrey was afraid to meet his eyes. She was afraid, because if he looked at her with disgust or disdain, she wouldn't be able to handle it.

After what felt like half an hour, but was probably only a couple seconds, Butator wrapped his arms around her and disrupted the heavy silence. "I believe that you believe that, but I think those are logical fallacies."

"They're what?"

"You're over generalizing, taking specific examples out of context, taking more responsibility than is yours and applying those outcomes to the rest of your life."

She wiggled her eyebrows, trying to wrap her head around what he'd just said.

"I'll explain later," he interrupted her thinking. "But right now, let's scope out one of these places before the others go in and mess up our investigation." He walked to the closet of the room that was built to be a bedroom and repurposed for his own uses. She saw him pull out a backpack, already full, and return to her like everything was normal.

"Can you take me to this one?"

CHAPTER 9

Butator and Audrey reformed on the roof of a grocery store across the street from their target. An office building with giant silver lettering above the door that read 'Pain Management Center.' Crouching, they both peered at it, searching for signs of activity, until Audrey saw what they were looking for. "It's warded against angels."

"Where? How can you tell?"

"You see that sticker on the bottom right of the door?" She waited until his head nodded. "The same one is in every window. I can't be a hundred percent sure, but I'd bet anything that's a ward."

Butator pinched his lips in frustration, then turned and began digging through his pack, pulling out project boxes, charging cables, external chargers, and small pelican cases as he went. "Alight," he muttered. "I'm going to need you to go in there." He opened a box and began pulling out a tiny camera and microphone. "Do you think you could get in there wearing a wire?"

"Sure," she agreed and returned to watching the door

of the building, spotting Asael and Isda strolling casually to the front door. "Look!"

Butator popped his head up and watched silently as the two angels from Gabriel's estate approached the motion-sensored door but stopped short of entering. They quickly altered their course around the side of the building where they had a small discussion then proceeded to circle the whole thing. Having given up on getting into the building they disappeared.

* * *

"Not there?" Gabriel questioned Asael. "Where would they have gone?"

Everyone had returned home with the same reports that the clinics were being warded, save for Ornias and Hamal. Ornias had gone in alone but didn't find anything.

Gabriel gave a sigh of exasperation. "Someone call him."

"On it," Ramatel answered.

"Where would he go?" Gabriel asked aloud again to no one in particular.

"Neither of them are answering their phones," Asael added.

Gabriel pursed his lips in frustration. "Does anyone know how he does that tracking thing with the cell phones?"

"Liwet might," Michael suggested. "He helped track Hamal for Ornias when they had their little escapade."

"That's right," Gabriel agreed, remembering back to that incident. "Get him in here."

* * *

Audrey walked calmly through the door of the clinic into an empty entry way housing an unmanned desk with a bouquet of fake pink, dusty flowers sitting in the middle of it. Beside that was a directory of office suites with the names of the various doctors and labs that were housed in the building. It looked like there were about twenty suites and she pondered how she was going to recon them. Finally she took a picture of the directory and walked to the elevator. *I guess I'm going to have to go one by one*, she thought with a sigh.

On the second floor she walked into the first office, scanning for signs of demonic activity, wards, hex bags, anything that could indicate that this was what she was looking for.

"Hi! Can I help you?" asked a seated woman in white scrubs.

Audrey studied her for a moment, scanning her for residual evil, scenting her, but the woman was clearly human. "I'm looking for Dr. Aleida."

"Oh sorry, dear, you have the wrong suite. Dr. Aleida is in the next office," the woman pointed to the right.

"My mistake. Thank you," Audrey answered and turned around, giving the area another visual sweep before leaving.

For the next hour, Audrey continued walking into the wrong office, checking each one for signs of evil, before thanking them for the redirection and moving on. She hoped they didn't have a building security officer watching her visit every suite on each floor.

Finally, when she was half way through the fourth floor, she walked into a suite labeled Pain Management for Chronic Back Pain. A wave of familiar energy washed over her with a chill down her spine when the door swung in, alerting her that she'd found her target, and she was greeted by a twenty-something blonde with a bob haircut and blue eyes. "Welcome to Pain Management," the woman said through a smile that looked like it was velcro'ed on. "Do you have an appointment?"

Audrey sniffed the air, flaring her nostrils a little, and looked around the room over the head of the seated woman.

No, not a woman, Audrey could smell the evil in her. This was a demon, albeit a very young one. Audrey fixed her eyes back on the blonde. "No, I'm a walk in."

"Oh, sorry, but you'll need to make an appointment, I'm afraid we don't take walk-ins."

"Why don't you go tell the doctor I'm here," Audrey suggested. "He might see me."

"Sorry but I can't do…" The woman stopped short when Audrey let her eyes go black and snarled at her.

"Like I said, go let him know."

The blonde scampered off like a scared rabbit through a door behind her, leaving Audrey alone to scope the place. She looked up at a camera in the corner that was trained on her and gave it a glare before scanning the rest of the place. The office was sterile white, typical medical office decor, with a desk and laptop where the secretary had been sitting. A hallway off to the right boasted six more closed doors, like a miniature hospital, with a linoleum white and gray tiled floor.

She was tense and wary but not nervous yet, still she wished she had her chains in case things got ugly. She also wished she had a plan.

CHAPTER 10

"The doctor will see you now," chirped the blonde with a fake smile, in what had to be her best impression of innocence.

Audrey rolled her eyes. "How about that," she retorted dryly and let herself be led down the hall to the second door on the right.

This small exam room had a hospital bed in a half upright position lined with white paper, a computer, another camera in the corner, a wheeled sitting stool, and a sink. The secretary deposited her and left with a "the doctor will be with you in a moment" through her stickered lips.

Audrey wished she could talk to Butator and tell him what was going on, but she didn't dare with that camera aimed at her.

Look natural, she told herself, trying to settle her discomfort. She seated herself on the exam table, letting her legs swing, glad she'd worn her combat boots in case she had to run or fight.

Momentarily the door knob spun and the door

opened to an attractive middle aged man with dark hair and tan skin. His slightly African features suggested mixed ethnicity, but it didn't really matter because the human form could have been just a meat suit. He shut the door and casually sat on the stool before addressing her.

"I'm doctor Florez, I hear you're having an emergency with back pain?"

Audrey snorted in response, but in a snap decision she did something she knew she wouldn't be able to undo.

She decided to take a chance, a big one. She could infiltrate this group, at least if Butator was right about her anyway. He believed in her, he thought she was smart and capable, and dare she even consider... good?

Was he right? Then again for that matter, had she ever known him to be wrong?

Take the chance, she told herself.

She reached under her shirt and disconnected the wire she was wearing.

She wasn't betting on herself though, she was betting on him.

"I WANT IN," Audrey declared to the 'doctor' seated in front of her.

The man tensed for about half a second, then, as though he remembered his cover, he widened his eyes, trying to portray confusion. "In? I don't understand. You are in the office already. Why don't you tell me about your back pain?"

She leaned back and crossed her arms in front of her. "Don't fuck with me." She let her eyes go to their naturally black state then back again. "I know about your operation here and the money you're sending to Mexico, and I want in."

"Who the fuck do you think you are?" he snarled, jumping up and allowing his own eyes to darken.

Audrey fought to remain calm. "I'm the one that can make or break this whole thing for you, but I want in and I want thirty percent."

The demon doctor huffed. "You must be high."

"You want this to last? You're going to need to go above ground. It's only a matter of time before someone catches your people dropping money all over. You need to go legit and launder the money the right way."

He gave her a dubious look. "And I suppose you're going to be the one to set that up?"

"Damn right. I have a lot of experience with this kind of thing. You can even check my references."

In a condescending tone, the doctor questioned, "And who might they be?"

"Agares, Zepar, and I've done some work for Seir too," she replied calmly, knowing that would get his attention.

He paused, reflecting on what she'd said, then "I can do all those things on my own," he answered, standing to walk out of the room.

"Yes, you can. But you don't have what I have access to."

"Your dick sucking lips ain't going to help you out this time, sugar."

Audrey snarled and launched herself at the door, slamming it shut just as he opened it. "I have a healing angel."

The man froze and studied her. "Who?"

"Her name is Isda. She's young and naive, and she'd buy whatever bullshit you sell her. You can keep her; make her heal for you so you can stay above ground, because if you're not actually delivering a measurable service, the humans will pick up on it eventually. You're a medical clinic; you need to actually heal some people."

Dr. Florez sat back down, deep in thought. "I'll consider the offer."

"You mean you'll ask permission from Mr. Catman in Mexico."

His eyes went wide again and he pursed his lips.

"I told you, I know all about your little operation."

He blew air out his nose. "How do we know you're legit?"

"I'll bring her to you within the hour," Audrey offered. "You can decide then, but I'm going to need something in return before I go."

"What's that?"

"I need a little tour of the office. I need to know that your operation is even worth my time. You might have just been lucky so far, selling whatever potion, whatever mind spell you're offering, because you sure as shit ain't that good."

He laughed. "It's no potion we're selling."

She raised an eyebrow. "Prove it."

Now he froze. "Bring me the angel, and I will. You show me yours, I'll show you mine."

"Fine. I'll be shredding your angel wards as I leave though."

He nodded and left the door.

* * *

Butator was worried about Audrey. He hadn't heard anything from her in about twenty minutes, and he was on the verge of texting the other angels when he saw her leave the building. She walked behind it, and then in a flash, she was back on his rooftop.

He felt the tension leave his shoulders when he saw her. "Are you alright? What happened?"

She crouched down and sat beside him. "I found the place, but I think they have something jamming the signal. Can you see where Isda is?"

"Sure," he said, pulling out a laptop. "Did you see anything in there?"

"Not really, but they're hiring so I'm going to bring Isda here to… have her" Audrey used air quotes with her fingers… "apply for a job." She lowered her hands. "It is definitely the right place though, but I couldn't get into the other rooms to see what they're hiding."

He opened an application on the screen and clicked on Isda's name. "Her phone is in her lab so as long as she is with it, she's there."

"Is she alone?"

One by one he clicked on everyone else's name. "Alone in the lab, but everyone else is back at the estate. I knew they wouldn't find anything."

She nodded in agreement. "Do they know where we are yet?"

"I haven't told them."

"OK good. I'm going to go get Isda, but I need you to do me a favor."

Butator smiled at her, glad he could do something of use. "What is it?"

"Don't tell them where we are yet, not until Isda and I come out of there."

"OK," he agreed, knowing he was already in trouble with the angels or at least that they'd be mad, but he trusted Audrey.

CHAPTER 11

Audrey reformed outside the walk-in gate that she had to use whenever she came and went without an angel. She punched in the code that released the gate, breaking the demon ward, with annoyance that she was now the only one so un-rehabilitated that she couldn't just walk through the wards like everyone else.

Once through, she flashed over to Isda's lab alone, the first and only time she'd ever actually been in there.

"Hey Isda," she called.

The other woman turned around, her chestnut hair spinning in the breeze like a ballroom gown. "Oh, there you are! The others have been looking all over for you and Butator."

"Yeah, I think we found something, but I need you to come with me, Butator is hurt," Audrey exclaimed, closing the distance between her and the angel.

Audrey grabbed Isda's wrist and vanished them from the spot, reappearing back in the exam room she'd been in with the doctor, now accessible to angels thanks to Audrey scratching out the warding design. "Stay here, I'll go get him."

Audrey stepped into the hall just in time to see Dr. Florez walking a patient that smelled human down the hall. A tilt of her head toward the door she was closing behind her was all the communication she offered. He deposited the woman in another office, promising to return in a moment.

"What the fuck are you doing back here?" he hissed as though trying to keep his voice down.

"I brought you the angel like we agreed."

Startled, he questioned, "So soon? Is it in there?" He looked at the closed door.

"Yes, but you'd better hurry. She thinks she is here to heal someone."

"And she just went with you willingly?"

"I told you, she'll buy anything."

A nurse emerged from another room, closer to the reception area, and he called to her as he briskly closed the distance, likely to avoid having Isda hear him. "Maggie, go fix the angel wards and get everyone over here right now! Bring a set of manacles, infused ones."

When he returned to Audrey she arched an eyebrow. "I believe you owe me a tour."

"After we secure the angel," he promised.

Soon, four new demons were waiting outside the door to the exam room, one held an open set of manacles. "Wait, get the human out of here," he ordered Audrey. She plastered on her best, professional smile, and walked into the exam room she'd seen the human enter.

After explaining an office emergency to the very confused and somewhat frustrated woman, Audrey deposited her outside the suite and was about to return to the exam room, when she heard a scuffle, followed by a scream, a hard object hitting a wall, maybe two, then she heard Isda calling her name.

Audrey took a deep breath to center herself. She'd expected this and she even thought she was ready for it, but listening to Isda's panicked screams tugged at her heart more than she'd anticipated. What was this sensation... guilt?

Guilt for hurting someone she didn't even like. Maybe she *was* rising.

Audrey braced herself for Isda's ire, and then stepped into the hall to see that they were moving her through another door.

Isda looked at her wide eyed and Audrey did nothing. Then Isda's expression darkened... Audrey had heard the phrase 'if looks could kill' before, but what she saw in Isda's face was more than that. It wasn't just the surprise, anger, and hatred she'd expected, it was the look of naivety being slaughtered, the end of innocence. It was a look that told her she was never coming back from this betrayal.

The door closed and the screaming was muffled, and then stopped.

Leaning against the wall, arms crossed, and an intentionally bored expression on her face, Audrey watched as one by one the demons emerged from the room, adjusting their clothing and resetting their hair, then returning to their business as if they hadn't just detained an angel.

Finally, the doctor emerged, rubbing at his face where it looked like Isda had landed a blow, and Audrey pushed off the wall. "Your turn."

He nodded his agreement, and then waved her over with one hand. She approached him, and followed the doctor through the door they'd pushed Isda through. The room was another exam room, though this held a dentist's chair rather than a bed. The far wall had a curtain drawn obscuring her view and she could hear Isda's muffled curses coming from a cleaning closet on the right.

The doctor strode across the room and with a swipe of his arm, he pushed the curtain aside, revealing a nightmarish hairy, human sized, monkey creature hanging from the ceiling by its feet. Its head appeared as a giant mosquito's with bulbous bug eyes, and needle-like beak the length of her arm protruding. It scurried away when the curtain was drawn, trying to hide from the light.

"Abúhukü?" Audrey asked, doing her best to sound nonchalant. "What are you doing with it?"

The doctor gave her a sly smile. "Feeding it of course, for a fee that is."

Audrey rolled her eyes. "Don't play coy; this is a potential business meeting. Explain the operation and I'll decide if it's worth my while. If it is, I may even introduce you to some... investors."

He picked up a clipboard from a counter and handed it to her. She glanced at the paperwork that appeared to be a traditional consent to medical treatment form. From the cleaning closet Isda's complaints ceased, as though she too wanted to hear the answer.

"Humans come in with pain and we introduce our latest medical technology." He gestured toward the ceiling that held a helmet connected to dozens of wires. Grasping it from where it hung above the chair he stretched it downward and pulled a flap from the top of it. "You see, the Abúhukü has to numb the victim, much like a mosquito before it eats, and the anesthesia lasts for weeks. Their pain is gone, and they pay us to do this."

A smudge mark on the paper drew her attention. "What is this?"

"The payment agreement."

She held the paper up and saw that what looked like an ink smudge was actually tiny writing, where they agreed to sell their souls.

Audrey twisted her lips. "Well played. And what is your annual income?"

"We haven't been in business a year yet, but we average about thirty souls a month and $25,000." He paused. "So, what can you offer me?"

"Well, first, a suggestion. After that thing's been fed, have the angel heal them. You won't get repeat customers, but repeat customers only offer money, not souls. Get word of mouth about a miracle cure and that will bring in new business."

"Noted."

"I can set up a presentation for you by the end of the week. I need to make some calls." she said, hurrying from the room before he could press her for more information. "I'll see you Friday."

She walked down the hall, confident that he was watching her back. She wanted to destroy the angel ward as she left, but she needed to not be caught. It might be safer if Ornias did it, she decided. If they saw her doing it, her cover would be blown, so she left the building and vanished to Butator's roof.

Butator returned home with Audrey, both of them landing in Gabriel's study, right in front of the desk Gabriel was seated behind. Before he could even take a look around the room to regain his surroundings Butator blurted out, "Isda is in a demon clinic, and we need to get her out of there." He rattled off the address from memory.

"It's warded against angels. I can break it but then we'll have…"

"Where is my wife?!" came the hostile voice of Asael, his pierced features twisting in his rage to make him look every bit the Angel of Punishment he'd been for so long.

"We're going to get her," Gabriel answered as Butator jumped in front of Audrey to save her from an assault that was no doubt coming.

"What's going on?" Michael asked, walking into the room casually as if nothing had happened.

"Get your sword," Gabriel answered, and without hesitation Michael vanished from the spot, as Gabriel spun back to Butator. "What's the address again?"

Michael reformed holding a plastic pirate sword as Butator repeated the address.

"Let's go." Gabriel reached for a letter opener resting on a pile of papers then disappeared.

They all reformed in the parking lot of the building, apparently uncaring if they were seen, Butator noticed as he and Audrey emerged from a crouching position behind a car.

"Where is she?" Asael demanded.

"Suite 311, but as soon as they see me break the seal at the door they'll know what's up so we are going to have to run up the stairs."

Michael pinched his lips together as if he didn't believe her. "311. Which side of the building is it on?"

"The right," she pointed.

"Are there any windows in the room she's being held in?"

Audrey thought back to the last time she'd seen the prissy angel. "She's in a cleaning closet, and the room has 2 windows. It also has one of those Abúhukü creatures in there too."

"Were the wards on the windows or built into the building itself?" Michael asked.

"Windows."

The Angel of Warfare turned to his twin brother. "Ready?"

In response Gabriel's letter opener elongated and grew with a brilliant flash, revealing a flaming sword that hurt the eyes to look at. In the same instant, he released his feathery white wings from human form. "Ready."

Michael and Asael followed suit with their own wings, Asael readying a dagger, and Michael freeing his own sword from its secret confinement.

"How many demons will be in there?" Michael asked. "Besides the Abúhukü."

"Probably not more than two."

"Gabriel and I will break the wards and hold off the Abúhukü. Asael you grab Isda and get her out of there." Michael turned to Butator and Audrey. "You guys stay down here as back up. If we try to go in through the front, that would give them too much of a warning. When you see us leave, you get back to the estate."

Without waiting for assent, they launched themselves into the air, beating their wings to propel them higher and away from the building. They turned like a formation of fighter jets, the flaming swords held before the Archangels, then shot towards the windows, swords first, crashing through, with Asael following immediately behind Michael.

"Holy shit," Audrey exclaimed as they punched through the wards. "They can do that?"

"If the wards are weak, and the angels are strong, they can."

She blew air out her mouth. "I'll bet those demons

never thought they'd be warding off the two most powerful angels on earth."

Butator chuckled and returned to watching the window in time to see Michael and Gabriel exiting, waving a signal for them to head home.

CHAPTER 12

"YOU BITCH!" Asael cried, dashing toward Audrey from across the study, only to be struck in the chest by lightning. He turned and glared at Barakel, who'd thrown the lightning bolt. "Don't get between us!"

"Don't make me," he slowly snarled back, hands still at the ready to throw another bolt.

"All of you calm the fuck down!" Gabriel commanded, walking into his office from the study.

"She abducted my wife and turned her over to the demons!" Asael yelled.

"Is Isda alright?" Gabriel asked calmly.

Asael seemed to relax a little at the question. "Yes, she's fine."

"Good, go get her and let's get to the bottom of what happened."

Audrey felt a sense of dread in her gut, knowing that she was going to have to look Isda in the eye, especially given the way Isda had looked at her the last time. She wished she could disappear and avoid this whole mess.

"Are you alright?" Barakel asked when Asael left.

She sighed. "Yeah, I'm fine. I'm just not looking forward to having to eat crow."

"Why would you eat a crow?" Butator asked. Looking at her like she was sprouting a second head as he joined her on the couch.

She chuckled. "It's just an expression for having to say you're sorry."

"Are you sorry?"

She shrugged. "Kind of."

Barakel and Butator both beamed at her.

"What?"

"You're rising," Barakel stated, joining them on the seat across the coffee table.

She scoffed. "I doubt it."

"If you were evil you wouldn't be sorry," he noted.

She paused and considered this, but before she could get too deep in thought, Asael and Isda walked in, hand in hand. It looked Isda had been crying, and Audrey averted her eyes.

"OK," Gabriel began as everyone gathered in the study. "Let's hear it."

Audrey and Butator explained what had happened and their rationale, but the lack of response as they continued gave her a sinking feeling that Butator didn't appear to share. He plowed through his version of the details as matter-of-factly as ever, as if he were recounting what he'd had for breakfast.

Audrey however noticed the hard stares with narrowed eyes and clenched fists and did her best to answer vaguely, but truthfully, although some of that only made it worse, so she just went back to Butator's tactic and finished telling the story.

When she said her last word she waited for the

response.

Gabriel started first. "Audrey, I understand what you were trying to do, but here we work as a team."

Isda interrupted him with something mumbled that ended with "itch." All eyes turned to her, especially since no one had ever really heard her curse before.

With her voice consistently rising in volume and violence Isda unleashed on Audrey. "You went in alone to determine what those things were, not telling anyone, and now they all know that we're onto them. They're probably cleaning house as we speak, and you had to use me…" she opened air quotes with her fingers, "because you needed them to believe I was scared! Well guess what?" She put her hands on her hips and leaned in with her eyes narrowed. "I was fucking scared! You had no right to make that decision for me and you don't know a damned thing about my acting skills! You…" She pointed a finger at Audrey, "Were being selfish and inconsiderate! This was all about your own ego!"

Audrey's initial reaction would have been to punch Isda in the face, but she knew she couldn't, deep down even she knew that was the wrong reaction. She wanted to defend herself from Isda's words, but she couldn't.

Isda was right.

Audrey was just being evil, because she was evil.

Because, that's all she was ever going to be.

She bit her lip to stop it from trembling and took a breath. Without meeting Isda's eyes, Audrey calmly replied. "You're right. I'm sorry."

Then she disappeared.

* * *

Audrey, extra annoyed that she had to stop at the gate

again to leave the estate, reformed somewhere in an alley in West Hollywood that smelled like rotting food and human excrement. It reminded her of hell, which couldn't be more appropriate if she'd searched for an odor.

Human shit. That's all I am and that's all I'll ever be. I tried to do the right thing and I fucked it up, like I fuck up everything! I'm a failure!

She turned to face the wall of the building nearest her in the alley and punched her fist into it, scraping the skin off her knuckles, then feeling it heal with her demonic powers immediately.

She punched out with her other fist, then over and over in rapid succession she punched until there was a hole in the wall and a puddle of her own black blood under it but she kept healing no matter how badly she hurt herself.

Maybe this is what hell really is.

She felt her knuckles pop back into place and skin regrow. A thought occurred to her then and she reached into her pocket. Retrieving her phone, she dropped it to the ground and stomped it into oblivion.

With a final scream of frustration she punched another hole in the wall with one hard punch, pissed that even in her attempt to hurt herself she couldn't do it.

Fuck! Fuck them all! I hate them! Every. Damn. One. I hate them all! They set me up to fail from the very beginning, all the way back. Set up to fail as a sister, as a person, as a demon, as an angel...

She went on punching as her thoughts spiraled out of control.

I'll never be one of them. Ever. I never am. They don't really want me, no one wants me, not the real me. Her mind flashed through her human life as a slave, and her times on earth in America, all the subtle and overt racism, the implicit message that she wasn't welcome.

Fuck them all!

Fine. If I'm destined to be evil, then so be it.

She pursed her lips and walked out of the alley, dripping black blood until her hands healed. She turned left on the sidewalk, walking briskly with the energy of her fury, her jaw set forward and her eyes glaring the hatred she felt for every living being on earth. The humans scattered out of her way like they recognized the danger she presented. Without attending to her direction, Audrey stalked the streets, hoping someone would challenge her because she needed to punish someone right now.

A few minutes into the walk, recognition of her location struck her. She was in front of that racist restaurant Butator had taken her to.

Perfect.

She wasn't entirely sure of what she was going to do yet, but she turned to head to the back of the building. It was early afternoon still, and the dinner crowd wouldn't be in there yet, but-

Getting out of her car was that stupid little hostess that had made her wait, until Audrey had lightened her skin, then, lo and behold, a table miraculously appeared. Audrey aimed straight for this blonde little twit.

"You!" she snarled, allowing her eyes to revert to their demonic black, and lifting her upper lip to bare her teeth that were morphing into fangs.

The girl glanced over, frozen momentarily with her jaw hanging open before she snapped out of it. The blonde dropped her purse and sprinted away with Audrey dashing after her. The human was no match for her, but she let the little blonde think she was, chasing her several blocks, watching her tire, then, out of desperation to hide, the human turned into a dumpster-lined alley that curved to the left. It must have resulted in a dead end because the human's grunts and breathing weren't audible anymore.

Audrey slowed to a brisk walk and rounded the corner, where the hostess was trying to scale a chain link fence topped with razor wire. With one hand, Audrey reached for the girl by the back of her head, snatching a fistful of hair and tugging the human off the fence.

"Do you remember me?" Audrey hissed into the girl's tear filled face.

Sobs were the only answer.

The lack of a response only pissed her off even more and Audrey shook the hostess like a ragdoll. "Answer me!"

"N-no. Please let me go," the blonde answered with a whimper.

"I'm the one you wouldn't seat when you thought I was Black, you racist piece of shit."

The girl whimpered again and Audrey brought her hand back, ready to strike the hostess's nose into the back of her brain.

"Wouldn't do that if I were you, honey," came a voice from the ground behind her.

The demon turned her head toward the speaker to see an elderly homeless Black woman with gray hair sticking out from under a baseball cap. She was pushing a shopping cart in front of the dumpsters like this was a shopping trip. The woman, still holding a dumpster lid open, retrieved a paper cup, tried the straw to see if there was any liquid remaining, before throwing the cup back in and digging for more.

"Mind your own damn business," Audrey answered and turned back to her work.

"Umm, hmm. Yes, ma'am, yes ma'am. I am minding my business, my business is stopping you from doing something you'll regret later," the woman replied, pulling her hand back with a new paper cup.

As Audrey watched the tramp try the straw again and

reject this cup too, a strange sensation came over her. When she focused on the woman now, Audrey could tell this was some kind of a celestial being; but whether demon or angel, she wasn't sure.

No, this was something else, something entirely different.

Audrey dropped the girl, who took off running, but didn't get a second glance from the demon.

"Who are you?" Audrey asked.

"Me?" the woman asked, turning around as if looking to see who else Audrey might be asking.

"Yes, you."

"Oh, I'm no one, don't you worry your pretty little head about that. I'm just looking for a drink."

Audrey studied her a moment, wondering if this was what happened to angels or demons that went crazy, and then she remembered what the woman had said. "What makes you think I'd regret hurting that little bitch?"

The woman turned to look Audrey up and down like she was inspecting a car she wanted to purchase, before finally answering. "Cuz it don't help and it won't solve anything."

Audrey snorted. "That's not true; it would make me feel better."

The transient lifted her eyebrows. "Would it?" She turned back to the dumpster and resumed fishing around for cups. "Or is hurting people the same kind of thing brought you here today?"

Audrey didn't answer, only glared at the woman, as she considered this. It was hurting Isda that had started all this, but the reminder of that just made her angry all over again. Hell, if she was honest with herself it was hurting people in general that led to her being here today. "Hurting people is what I'm good at."

"And how's that working out for you?"

Audrey narrowed her eyes. "It's working just fine, thank you very much," she snapped.

The woman retrieved yet another Styrofoam prize. "It's going to get you sent to the pit."

"Been there," Audrey answered and turned to leave.

"And got out I see." The elderly woman put her lips around a straw and sucked until it made gurgling noises. "Even made it to a cushy mansion in Beverly Hills."

"How'd you know that?"

The woman just shrugged and tossed the cup back. "I know things, people be talking when they don't think anyone's around to hear them. So you going to give all that up, just to hurt this little girl?"

"Don't you get it? That's who I am!"

"So be someone else."

"Why is it always *me* that has to be better? Why isn't it them? For once, just once why don't they ever get punished?

"Maybe they do later, but that's their business. Your business is what you do.

"So I'm just supposed to shut up and take it?"

"No, ma'am, that ain't what I'm saying at all."

"What are you saying then? Please enlighten me," she started sarcastically. "Because... I'm so sick of it all! I've been used and discarded, overlooked and underappreciated, and put down, and beat up my whole life! And every time I try to do something about it, I..." she pointed to her chest, "get punished! I was a slave and when I did something about it, I" she pointed to her chest again, "Was sent to the pit. I was the one who was the victim and yet I got punished!"

The homeless woman's expression softened. "You sure that's why you were sent there?"

Slightly thrown off by the question, Audrey asked. "What?"

"Are you sure that's why you were sent to the pit?"

How strange it was to have a conversation about celestial affairs with a ragged old homeless woman in an alley, but also a little relieving to be able to talk about it.

"What else could it have been?"

"Maybe, it was less about what you did and more about what you would have done if you hadn't gone there."

Audrey raised an eyebrow and the woman continued. "Can you honestly say you weren't a threat to anyone after that, carrying all that anger around?"

Audrey didn't answer because that woman was right and she didn't want to admit it. Inwardly she cringed. She was a threat to everyone and everything after that, and had been ever since.

"You're mad because life ain't fair, aintcha?"

Audrey clenched her jaw and looked away.

"Life ain't fair," the woman stated flatly. "You walking around here thinking life should be fair and driving yourself mad, but life ain't fair. Nothing in life is fair, not even in nature. You think it's fair to the deer when the wolf kills it? Is it fair to the wolf that it goes hungry? Life ain't fair, but haven't you ever heard that phrase, 'If you don't heal what hurt you, you'll bleed on folks who didn't cut you?'"

The woman paused before continuing. "Look, maybe you were justified in killing that slave owner, some folks just gotta die, but one thing I know for sure is that evil is an addiction. You were a victim forced to drink its elixir and it's been tainting your soul ever since. It might not be your fault that it got in there, but you have a responsibility to flush it out, and if you shirk that responsibility, you're going to make the same mistakes over and over again." She gestured to the fence that Audrey had pulled the girl off. "And keep landing yourself in the pit."

Audrey didn't reply. She couldn't yet because she was processing the information still, deciding whether to challenge it or incorporate it.

"I'm not saying you should just let injustice happen, I am saying that sharing that elixir of evil just spreads it around. Maybe you can do better, maybe you're too far... far... gone, but that choice is yours to make. Life ain't fair, but thinking in 'shoulds,' means you ain't living in reality!" The woman clapped her hands to emphasize the point. "You're living in an ideal world where everything is perfect, where it should be this way or that way, but life ain't like that. You've got to accept reality to change it. It ain't fair. You were hurt and you're hurting still, but you get to decide what to do about it now, and if you don't change, nothing else is going to change either."

Audrey was dumbfounded as she stood there staring into the dirty face of the vagabond. Finally, she opened her mouth and asked, "You don't think it's too late for me?"

The old woman smiled, revealing several missing teeth and a few brown ones. "It's never too late to start over."

Audrey pondered for another moment, then feeling the urge to respond just to fill the silence, she said, "I need to think about this."

"You take your time, honey. I'll leave you to it, but remember, how you got here isn't your fault, but where you go from here is your choice." With that, the woman began to dissolve into thin air, leaving behind a void. It was like life and love had been in front of her the whole time without her knowing it and now their absence was so tangible that Audrey felt tears welling in her eyes.

Somehow, she knew without a shadow of doubt, that she'd just had a conversation with God.

CHAPTER 13

With distress, Butator watched Audrey disappear from the room, knowing that he was powerless to stop her. She was in pain and she would retreat into hiding, but the scary part was that he wasn't sure when, if ever, she would re-emerge. He glanced at Barakel whose concerned expression told him that her grandfather was equally concerned.

The talking went on around them with urgency about how to destroy the demons at all the other clinics and the mansion in Mexico before word spread, but Butator wasn't really paying attention to the plan. He'd pulled his phone out to track Audrey's position, while Barakel joined him peering at the screen.

"Shit."

"What is it?" Barakel asked.

"Her phone is dead or off," he answered.

"Is there any other way to track her?" Barakel asked, his voice almost pleading with worry.

"Maybe." Butator started for the door to the study,

oblivious that he was walking through the middle of the planning, and beckoned for Barakel to join him.

"Where are you going?" Gabriel called.

"To find Audrey."

Asael scoffed like he wanted to say something, but Barakel raised a hand ready to throw a lightning bolt and silenced the pierced angel immediately. Gabriel too appeared as if he considered protesting, but thought better of it.

"Fine, but we will need you two when we take the mansion. Be ready, we'll be back after the clinics have been purged."

Butator nodded then practically ran for his own office. He felt like a part of him was broken and the person he wanted to talk to about the broken part was the broken part. She was hurting and he could do nothing about it. What if she was in trouble? What if she did something bad and the angels never let her return? He wanted to tell her that she'd done nothing wrong, or if she had it was alright because her intentions were good. Butator knew she was good, Barakel knew it too, but the others just didn't see it. They never gave her a chance. He'd been so close to proving it to her and then this.

Oh God, what if I never see her again?

"Do you know where she would have gone?" Barakel asked.

"No, but I can check some places." Butator threw himself into the desk chair and began clicking like a madman to start his tracing program.

"Fuck!"

Barakel's eyes widened in response.

"She's destroyed the SIM card in her phone."

Snatching his phone from his pocket he typed on the

tiny keyboard then held it up in front of Barakel. "Can you take me here?"

Barakel placed a hand on Butator's shoulder and vanished them both to the hilltop where Butator and Audrey had made love, unbeknownst to Barakel.

The hilltop was empty, and Butator directed Barakel to take him to the only places he'd shared with Audrey, to no avail. They searched the Jamaican restaurant, the Italian restaurant, and for some reason Barakel even suggested they search a sex club saying only that he'd heard that she'd been there before.

Finally, on the verge of tears, Butator returned home with Barakel. "Now what?" he asked, but Barakel only shook his head and sat down.

"I don't know," he answered, putting his head in his hands.

In that moment Gabriel walked in. "Did you find her?" he asked.

Butator didn't trust himself to answer; he only glared at Gabriel as though his anger could pierce the man through looking. He had been a part of those who'd driven her away, who'd doubted her. Butator clenched his fist, and turned away.

"No," Barakel answered, though his voice too sounded strained.

"I'm sorry," Gabriel offered. "But we will need you two with us to take the mansion. The clinics have been cleared out but we need to move fast before they alert them that we are coming."

At first neither Barakel nor Butator moved. *Audrey should be with us for this, it's her case too*, he thought, remembering back to her finding the location with him. Then his brain recalled the look in the man's eyes when his life ended as Butator watched through the window.

Yes, I have to help with this.

Butator stood, preparing to go with Gabriel, feeling the heavy gaze of both men on him.

"Thank you," Gabriel said, but Butator only shook his head.

"I'm not doing it for you," he answered, watching as Barakel rose to join them.

* * *

As Butator took his position along the outer wall that encircled the estate in Mexico, he tried to focus on the task at hand instead of Audrey. Internally he was arguing with himself, and somewhere between 'she's a grown woman who can take care of herself,' and 'she already thought badly of herself and now this happened, she'll be using this to confirm all those negative beliefs. She's never coming back, she doesn't love me.' He waited for the signal to attack.

The signal came when Michael and Gabriel together began hacking at the angel ward. From the wall a surge of power hit him at what must have been their initial slice at it, then a dip in presence of prohibiting force. Another surge told him they were trying again and the ward was trying to protect itself like a living thing. On the third attempt, they killed it and he could sense it had died.

Barakel was in his peripheral vision to the right, Sahariel to his left, and both began to advance their approach. He too leapt to the top of the wall with them. They landed on the lawn and stalked toward the estate, weapons drawn. On high alert, he prepared himself for the possibility of danger, and fell in line along the house wall behind Barakel and Sahariel when they reached the door on this side of the estate. Barakel held up his fingers to give them a countdown to breach time.

3...2...1

Bang!

Barakel breached the door with lightning, blowing it into the room, and dashing in after it. Butator and Sahariel followed, taking different angles and clearing the house room by room as they ventured further inside.

Each room they entered contained all the threat of impending death, and each time they cleared one, calling the all-clear in their own directions, and receiving it from others. Butator could hear the other teams of three mimicking their actions from other entry points. Finally, they advanced upstairs continuing their clearance and cover-hopping with each other as they went.

"Butator!" Gabriel's voice came from downstairs, as they neared the final room. "It's all clear, get down here."

Butator heard him, but shook his head to the others, pointing at the room where he'd seen the man bludgeoned to death.

"You should go," Sahariel whispered.

"This one first," he insisted.

Sahariel nodded and gestured with a nod of his head for Butator to get behind him as they stacked up again outside the door. Butator's heart was pounding, expecting the murderer to be inside waiting for them, a trap having been set. Would the body still be there?

Bang!

They poured into a bedroom, tidy and neat, save for the dark brown blood stain on the hardwood floor.

It was empty.

Butator sighed. "This was where that guy was killed," he pointed to the stain.

No one said anything, they simply nodded and were

quiet as if expecting something from him, but he wasn't sure what.

"Let's go find the others," Sahariel suggested finally.

* * *

"The place has been cleared out. They must have known we were coming," Gabriel called as they approached. No one needed to say more, but he was aware that they all mentally added "Fucking Audrey," to that.

Gabriel faced Butator. "Can you open this door?"

Behind Gabriel was a grey metal door with a keypad entry system that would have been more suited to a military bunker. He inspected the keypad device and calculated the number options in his head. A closer inspection of the keys revealed that only four of them were used regularly. They were polished with grease from fingers where the rest had dust.

"Yes," he answered simply, and got to work trying number combinations.

CHAPTER 14

Audrey replayed those final words in her head as she stood in the alley, shadowed by the building around her. "How you got here isn't your fault, but where you go from here is your choice."

Where do I go from here?

When she'd left the estate she'd never planned to go back, she figured she might try another country.

But, could she go back? She pictured herself returning, metaphorical tail between her legs. What would the others say? It would be so tense and hostile between herself and Isda and Asael.

Then she pictured Butator and remembered him putting himself between Asael and her, and Barakel electrocuting his friend for her with a lightning bolt.

She smiled at the thought. Maybe she could do this.

She vanished from the spot and reformed outside the walk-through gate and let herself onto the estate property. Behind her a rush of wind and buzzing sounded in the bushes that lined the property, causing her to spin on her heels.

And right into the blow that knocked her unconscious.

*   *   *

Audrey was vaguely aware of being dragged into the mansion, and up the stairs, but her vision was tunneled and blurry, and her mind felt like someone was rapidly flipping through channels but wouldn't land on a single one. As they reached the landing of the stairs the flipping was slowing down enough for her to acknowledge that there were four or five demons in human form, and that two of them had her by the arms.

As if the layout had already been given to them, the other three marched into Isda's lab, and Audrey heard the young angel scream. Jahi, who must have been babysitting, stuck her head out into the hall, and then vanished when she saw the danger. *Good, she'd tell the others. They'll be here any second.* With that thought, she felt her legs wobble and let her eyes close.

The sound of gurgling water was the first thing she noticed next. She opened her eyes to see that they were in a room made of concrete that had been painted over with a tan color and bore wardings that she wasn't familiar with, written in blood. On one side a large black jaguar lounged on an elegant sofa, and an enormous fish tank occupied the back wall, but she couldn't see any fish. Just worms. There was a dentist's chair in the center of the room and another giant mosquito-monkey bobbed up and down excitedly in the corner, a loud buzzing coming from its wings.

Isda, still struggling and screaming despite the chains wrapped around her, fought the demons that were carrying her, but then the men dropped her to the floor with both a loud thud from the chains, and a grunt of pain from Isda.

She whimpered, the sound of which was pitiful and gut wrenching.

Audrey tried to move only to find her arms were bound with what had to be heavenly infused shackles, so even her demon strength couldn't help her now. With her senses returning, she was starting to appreciate the danger of the situation. Both of them were bound, surrounded by demons, and she guessed no one knew where to find them.

Fuck, we're in trouble now.

"As you requested," one of the men who'd just dropped Isda announced to the cat.

"Good. Go take care of the commotion outside the door."

The demon just nodded and gestured to a couple of them to follow him, and they disappeared.

The cat turned around and shifted to human form, then pulled a silk robe from a hook on the wall. "You didn't really think we'd fall for that little ruse of yours did you, Audrey? I've got more connections in hell than you'd ever imagine, and if we're being honest, your references don't check out."

She swallowed hard but didn't answer, because she was actually feeling around for something to try to pick her lock with.

Hurry!

Her fingers landed on something small and hard, and she began to explore as the robed man turned around.

"You were right about one thing though."

Buy time! Stall him.

"Oh, what was that?" She responded, trying to sound casual.

"We do need her." He pointed at Isda.

"What for?" Audrey asked. She didn't care; she just needed to keep him talking while she was working.

"For my pets of course! Her energy will feed them for eternity and I'll be able to hatch thousands of them! No, millions!" His face came alight, looking beyond the women and at the tank of worms in water.

"Gross," she answered before she could stop herself.

"Gross you say? Have you seen the human race?"

From the corner of the room, a metal door began beeping, and then buzzing each time the code failed. With every new attempt that was made, the buzzing would indicate a failure, but the beeps she heard with the tries were fast, too fast for human fingers. *Inwardly she smiled to herself.*

"Ugh," the demon scoffed and rolled his eyes. "Bothersome." He crossed the room, yanked Isda up to her feet, and started to drag her to the chair. The mosquito being in the corner hummed louder as he drew near, raising the intensity of the moment with its volume.

"Get your hands off me!" Isda screamed at the demon, and then tried to bite him, scoring herself a backhand for the effort that knocked her head to the side.

"Isda?" the voice came from outside the door. Someone began to pound on the door as if trying to break it down with a battering ram, but the demon seemed nonplussed.

Isda was roughly pressed into the chair and wrapped tightly with chains across her midsection.

Audrey watched in horror as the beast approached the angel from behind then lowered its giant needle-like stem to her head. Isda thrashed violently, until the cat demon raised the bumpers on either side and threw another chain over her forehead.

Audrey felt the pain of her own skin breaking as she pulled against the manacles holding her. *Maybe I can use my blood as lubrication to slip out.* She pulled harder and harder, feeling the strain in the muscles of her shoulder and arms now, along with the sharp burning in her wrists, but nothing compared to the pain she felt when Isda screamed as the monster's needle penetrated her skull.

At that sound, with one final burst of energy, Audrey snapped the manacles and sprang to her feet, blood dripping from her wrists. She tried to throw herself at the beast drinking from Isda but the man stepped into her path knocking her aside with a blow, then he shifted to jaguar form.

Audrey tried again, only to be pounced on by the cat, but this time, urged on by Isda's whimpers and cries, she fought like a banshee, first gouging at its eyes then kicking it off her with a cry of exertion.

She'd only have a second before it bounced back but maybe that was all she needed. She lunged for the monster, throwing her weight against it with her shoulder, and successfully knocking it off balance. Then she did the only thing she could think of, just as the door burst open and Butator and Asael were about to dash in.

She put her hands on Isda and vanished them both from the spot.

* * *

"Audrey! Get back here!" Butator heard Asael scream in frustration. They'd both just seen Audrey take Isda again, but they didn't have time to worry about that right now.

"What happened?" Gabriel called as he dashed past Butator and struck at one of the demons that tried to protect the insect-like being.

Asael turned to respond then saw the attack from their rear just as Barakel was turning to face it. "Behind you!"

Lightning bolts, smoke, and loud cracks filled the corridor they'd once occupied as the angels all took to fighting the demons in the room or those trying to advance on their rear.

As the angels fought with swords and knives, and any other weapons at their disposal, no one noticed the cat-man scratching a symbol into the wall with a clawed finger, until Asael managed to behead the demon protecting its leader, and grabbed the man by the throat.

Finally, when all was said and done, only the cat demon remained of the evil horde, though he too was backed into a corner.

"Where are they?" Asael snarled at the demon, who now stood with his chin up to avoid the blade at his throat.

The demon laughed. "I have no idea, but I'll give you a piece of advice. Never trust a demon."

With a cry of frustration, Asael plunged his knife into the demon's neck then quickly retracted it, letting the body fall to the floor, as he spun to face Butator. "Where is she?"

Butator could see the anger and fear written on the face of the pierced angel who was searching again for his wife, and he wished he could reassure him, but he knew that was futile. He wracked his brain for where Audrey might have taken Isda, so he said the first thing that came to his mind.

"She probably took her home."

"If she's not there…"

A lightning bolt flew past Asael's head as a warning not to finish that sentence. Asael just shot Barakel a sideways glance, and vanished.

"You two go home too, and try to find them," Gabriel said, using a chin nod to indicate Butator and Barakel. "We'll stay here and finish up. Barakel can you keep Asael in line?"

"Yeah, he's no problem."

"I'm going too," Philotanus added, always protective of Barakel.

"Fine."

When they reformed back at the estate, all they could hear was Asael running room to room calling for his wife.

"Where is she?" he called to someone unseen upstairs.

"The demons took her!" Jahi's voice answered.

CHAPTER 15

Audrey reformed with Isda in the same back alley filled with dumpsters and stinking of rot. As she gently laid Isda's body on the ground, she could see the angel's brain through the golden blood and clear cerebral fluid that leaked out of a golf ball sized hole in her head.

"Lady! Transient! Where are you?" Audrey called.

The old woman emerged from beside a dumpster, that Audrey hadn't seen there a moment ago. "You looking for me?" she asked. This time she was wearing a shower curtain around her like a shawl and had torn, soiled lamp shade upside down on her head like a crown.

"Yes! Can you help her?"

The woman looked at Isda. "She don't need my help, she's healing on her own, look."

Audrey glanced at the hole in her head and found that it was shrinking, and then chastised herself for forgetting that Isda was the Angel of Healing.

Relief still flooded through her and she felt her shoulders drop, as she sat back on the ground by Isda's head.

For a moment they were silent, waiting for the healing to progress, but as it did Audrey felt a growing sense of unease as she wondered what to expect from Isda when she woke up. She didn't have to wait long before the hole closed and hair began growing over it.

Isda sat up and felt the back of her head, then looked around at her surroundings, saying nothing. Her eyes landed on Audrey and they sat in silence as Audrey waited for the just assault.

She could hear it already in her head, as though she'd heard it thousands of times before. "You good for nothing piece of shit. You let the demons into the estate, and let them take me! You shouldn't even have come back. You should have never come back. We don't want you! You're scum! You're a piece of shit! You're worthless, stupid, evil, pathetic…"

"Thank you," Isda interrupted the rant of abuse in Audrey's head, so softly that Audrey almost missed it, and then had to mentally replay it to make sure she'd heard correctly.

"What?" she asked in disbelief.

"Thank you," she repeated louder this time, and rubbed her head again.

The old woman crouched down and smiled, revealing her lack of dentistry visits for what must have been decades. "I SEE YOU'VE MADE YOUR DECISION AFTER ALL," she said in a voice that was no longer human, but had a power to it that reverberated throughout her body.

Audrey nodded, mostly because she wasn't entirely sure how to address the deity in a shower curtain, while Isda immediately rolled over and dropped her head down. She wondered if she was supposed to do the same thing, but then again, that wasn't really the kind of relationship she had with this being.

"WELCOME TO THE HEAVENLY RANKS, AUDREY," the woman spoke, then appeared to dissolve into the air, leaving the two of them alone in wonder.

Isda started to sit up, looking around for the woman. "You brought me to God?" she whispered in awe.

Audrey shrugged, but felt a blush crawling up from her neck. "Safest place I could think of."

Before she knew it, Isda's arms were around her, and Audrey first stiffened, preparing for an attack, until she noticed that this was a hug.

A hug. How strange it felt, but also warm, and welcoming.

"Isda," Audrey spoke feeling like she needed to clear something still. "I'm sorry for what I did earlier. I hurt you, and scared you... and got us into the mess."

Isda pulled back from the embrace and looked at Audrey. "Maybe everything happens for a reason," she said with a smile. "Let's go home."

Audrey rubbed awkwardly at her wrists that were also healing but at a slower rate than Isda's head had. The angel noticed and hovered her hands above the wounds, letting the light emitting from them speed the recovery.

Inwardly, Audrey was recalling the look on the faces of Butator and Asael as they burst through the door just in time to see Audrey disappear with Isda. "Yeah, about that, maybe you should go home first and explain things. I don't think I'm welcome there at the moment."

Isda smiled. "Alright, I can do that, but do you promise to wait here for me to return if I do?"

"I promise."

When Isda disappeared, Audrey stared out into the void where the transient had been. "You still there, Lady?"

The woman returned, though now she looked like a completely healthy version of the homeless woman Audrey had met. Her hair was neatly braided; she wore a healthy flush on clean skin, and smiled with the most beautiful smile Audrey had ever seen.

Recognition of the face from before tugged a memory from so long ago Audrey thought it had died. This was her mother. The woman she hadn't seen since she was taken from Africa.

Audrey's mouth fell open. "Mama?"

"Yes, child," her mother answered in their native language.

Audrey stood and walked into her mother's waiting embrace, feeling the warmth of love flood her as years of pain poured out of her in the form of tears. There was so much she wanted to say. Decades of stories to tell her, but the only words she managed after long moments of trying to catch her breath, were "Mama, I'm so sorry. I..." she struggled to breathe through the sobs that shook her body, "I... couldn't save him."

"Shh baby. Don't blame yourself for things that you couldn't control. You were a child too. And besides, he's here." With a wave of her arm, Audrey's brother appeared next to her, as fit and splendid in his tribal attire as he ever was, and the smile that he held for her was radiant. She embraced him too and felt like someone was pouring gold into the cracks of a broken vase, using the fractures to create art as they mended the ceramic.

No one spoke, Audrey merely appreciated the presence and feel of the others, unsure if she could even speak if she wanted to, until she felt the familiar sensation of an angel forming behind her.

She turned to see that Barakel and Butator had taken shape behind her in the alley. They smiled, genuinely happy to see her safe and loved, but neither moved to interrupt the reunion. Audrey looked at the faces of her new family, then back at those of her old. "Come on," she said to her mother and brother. "There are people I want you to meet."

EPILOGUE

Audrey sat across from Butator in his office, sipping coffee and playing on her phone as usual, when a news headline disrupted her scrolling. Recognizing the name of the restaurant it was referring to, she clicked it open and read the article.

"Huh," she exclaimed. Butator stopped typing to look at her.

"That restaurant we went to was bought out last week, and was burned to the ground yesterday. Investigators say it was struck by lightning." She watched Butator's face, intent on catching any subtle indications that he or Barakel were behind it, but even as she did she realized the folly in her plan. Emotional facial expressions were still rare for him, and she'd learned to accept his words at face value.

"Oh."

"Did you have anything to do with that?"

He fidgeted a little this time before answering. "Yes. We donated the insurance money to the local food bank."

"Did you do that for me?" she asked incredulously.

"No, you have no need to visit a food bank," he

replied, then paused as he thought for a moment. "We may have done it because you exposed them, but not for you. I was thinking about it, and the only way to really stop racism is to ensure humans see each other as people, not just others, but we can't directly intervene, so instead if we do what we can to fight the oppression from the overall system, maybe it can take off from there."

He went back to typing as though he'd just explained how he likes his coffee, while she sat taking in his words. Finally, she stood up and walked over to him, giving him a kiss on the cheek. He stopped typing and smiled. "I just want you to know that I love you," she said.

His smile grew and he turned to look her in the eye, a new tendency that was reserved for her alone so far. "I love you too."

The End.

ABOUT THE AUTHOR

USA Today bestselling author Joel Crofoot was raised in northern New York state on a large family sheep farm, then left home to join the United States Marine Corps at 18 years-old. After spending four years in Japan as a radio operator, Joel re-enlisted into the bomb squad (explosive ordnance disposal) and was stationed out of California. Two tours to Iraq later, Joel decided to leave the Marine Corps to pursue higher education and graduated with a doctorate in psychology in 2017. After working several years in a community clinic, Joel went into private practice.

READ MORE FROM JOEL

* * *

Sign up for Joel's Newsletter

https://sendfox.com/JoelCrofoot

Made in the USA
Monee, IL
18 September 2023